Håkan Lindquist
MY BROTHER AND HIS BROTHER

Håkan Lindquist was born in Oskarshamn, a small harbor town on the southeast coast of Sweden; it is the setting for his debut novel, the critically acclaimed *My Brother and His Brother*. The book received a literary award – *Prix Littéraire de la Bordelaise de Lunetterie* – in 2002, when it was first published in France. Lindquist has written six novels, several short stories and one opera libretto. His novels and short stories have been translated and published in several European countries. *My Brother and His Brother* is the first of his novels to appear in English.

MY BROTHER AND HIS BROTHER

a novel by
Håkan Lindquist

Translated from the Swedish by the author.

BRUNO GMÜNDER

My Brother and His Brother
Copyright © 2017 Bruno Gmünder GmbH
Kleiststraße 23-26, 10787 Berlin, Germany
info@brunogmuender.com

Original title: Min bror och hans bror
Copyright © Håkan Lindquist 2002

Translated from the Swedish by the author
Copyright © Håkan Lindquist 2010

Cover art: Frank Schröder
Cover photo: Copyright © Howard Roffman
www.HowardRoffman.com

Printed in Germany

ISBN: 978-3-95985-252-4

More information about Bruno Gmünder books and authors:
www.brunogmuender.com

"Eternity is in love
with the productions of time."

—William Blake
"The Marriage of Heaven and Hell"

To the memory of my beloved brother Arne

Håkan Lindquist

1

There are five hundred and two days between the last day of your life and the first day of mine. Still, you have always been present, more or less.

My first true image of you was the school photograph that used to stand on top of the television in the living room. You are a thirteen-year-old boy who looks like my mother. Your hair is rather long, well groomed and dark. Just like Mother's. You don't smile in the picture. You don't look at me. Instead, your eyes are focused on something far beyond the camera and the schoolmates. I am an almost three-year-old boy standing in front of the television set looking up at your picture. The balcony door by my side is open. Flakes of snow find their way into the warmth. They whirl around your picture before they reach the floor and melt.

"Who's that?" I ask my parents.

"It's your brother," Mother replies, closing the balcony door. "It's your brother Paul."

"He died before you were born," Father explains.

But I'm cold and much too small to understand.

I am looking at your picture. Sometimes, if I'm sad, it seems you are sad too. When I'm happy, I believe I can see a secret smile on your lips.

I was standing there looking at the picture of you. I couldn't comprehend that you were my brother and that you were dead. It was a thought much too abstract for me. My family meant Mother, Father, and myself. You were still just a thought. Or, maybe, a wish.

When I grew older—this must have been when I started to school—I began to ask my parents about you. I wanted to know who you were, what you had done, with whom you had played. For you must have played, Paul, you were just a child when you died.

"Paul was so nice," Mother told me. And she was using the voice she'd use when she told me stories. "He was so clever. He liked painting and drawing. Everybody liked him. The teachers at school, the schoolmates, the kids on the street. They all liked him. And they were all so sad when he died, so very sad."

"Did all his classmates come to the funeral?" I asked.

"No. Not all. Just some of his closest friends. They'd had some ceremony at school already—I believe it was the day before the funeral—but the church was still full."

"Why did he die?"

"You know why," she said slowly. "I've told you a hundred times."

"But still," I begged. "I want you to tell me just once more. I want to hear it."

"He was hit by the train and died instantly. It was all very sudden."

"No," I said. "Not like that. Tell me like you used to tell me."

"Paul liked to go to the forest. He loved watching the animals and the flowers and trees. He was always hoping he'd meet some wild creature—"

"Did he ever meet fox cubs?" I interrupted.

Mother smiled. "Yes, one morning when he was up very early. Stefan and I had just waked up when Paul got home. He was laughing and yelling when he came through the door. 'Wake up! Wake up!' he yelled and entered our bedroom. He sat down on the side of the bed and began telling us about the fox cubs."

"How old was he then?"

"Eleven or twelve, I guess. And he told us about his walk in the forest. He had sat down on some old fallen tree-trunk when suddenly he heard a whining sound. At first he got scared, he told us, but he was so curious. So Paul climbed up on a big rock so that he could see better, and so that he would be safe, I guess. And right there, just below the big rock, he saw the three little fox cubs playing outside their burrow."

"That must have made him happy, didn't it?"

"Yes," said Mother, sounding a bit sad. "It made him very happy.

"The day he died he was also out in the forest. In the morning, at breakfast, he told us he'd go for a long walk. He hoped he would see something new, something he'd never seen before. I made him a sandwich and gave him a thermos with something to drink. And before he left I reminded him of the compass. In case he got lost. 'Cause the forest at the other side of the road is very large, you see."

"What happened next?"

"Then ... then Paul did something very dangerous, something you must never do. Remember that. You see, he got up on the railroad track, and when the train came he was thinking of something else. Maybe he had spotted an animal or something. And so he didn't hear the train, and he was hit, and died."

"Did it hurt?" I asked.

Mother shook her head. "I don't think it did. It was so sudden. And then, you don't have time to feel any pain."

After a while she continued, but now her voice was different.

"It was the twenty-first of July the year before you were born," she said, but it sounded as if she were talking to herself. "It was, by the way, the first day man walked on the moon. I remember feeling distressed in the early afternoon. Uneasy, in some way. Stefan was out in the kitchen washing the dishes. He had the radio on, and he was singing along with a song they played quite often that summer. *It's the time of the season, when your love runs high ...* ' And then the doorbell rang. I opened the door, and two policemen were standing there. They asked to come in.

"I didn't understand why they had come until we all stood in the kitchen. 'Has something happened to Paul?' I asked. One of the officers looked down at the floor. The other one nodded and said, 'Your son has been involved in a very serious accident.' But I still couldn't understand what he'd said. The radio was on. He told us Paul was dead. I yelled out: 'Turn off the bloody radio!' Then suddenly it was all so quiet, so horribly quiet. All I could hear was Stefan sobbing."

After Mother's story the apartment wasn't quite the same. It felt different. Almost unreal.

Imagine this, I've had a brother who has lived here, in this place we call our home. A brother who has moved around in this apartment, who has laughed and played here. A brother who has talked with my mother and my father, and spent a great deal of time with them.

Imagine this, I've had a brother who once lived in the room I call my own.

When I was still a child I used to take Paul's picture down from the television set. I looked at it carefully, held it close to my eyes, trying to see something new, something I had never seen before. Sometimes I took the picture with me into my room so that *he* could see, so that he could recognize himself. Because I had inherited not only Paul's room, but also his furniture, his toys and books, and even some of his clothes.

When I learned to read and write, I used to write about my brother on small pieces of paper. Here and there I can still find small notes with awkward letters and numbers.

Paul to Jonas—502 days. Or: *There are 12,048 hours between you and me.*

In the margin of my seventh-grade book in English I have written: *You are seventeen months away.*

I don't remember all my childhood thoughts of Paul, I only remember I thought of him often and that he felt very present most of the time. Sometimes we melded and became one and the same. And it felt as if I was he even then, even during his lifetime. It was as if it were I who—in a dream or some distant time—had seen the fox cubs outside their burrow that early morning. It was I who had been all too occupied with looking into the large forest on the other side of the road to notice the onrushing train. It was I who had died. It was I who was born

11

again—almost resurrected—seventeen months later. And yet, it was also you, Paul. All the time.

Sometimes I wish I had kept a diary when I was younger, but I never did. That is why the written evidences of my brother's presence to me during my childhood are nothing but scraps of paper with notes about the time that divides our lives.

When I was born 722,880 minutes had passed …

When I stopped writing notes about Paul, I still thought of him a lot, but he didn't feel very close anymore. It was as if he were fading away. Then something happened, and he was once again coming closer.

It was a few days before my sports holiday in the eighth grade. I had applied for a table-tennis tournament in the school gym, but only some days before my first game I happened to smash my paddle.

"Damn!" I grumbled, looking at the broken handle. "I can't afford a new one. Damn!"

Father was tired and irritated when I got home. He was sitting in the living room reading one of his fishing magazines. I showed him my paddle and told him what had happened.

"You're so clumsy," he said peevishly. "You always break things."

"I do not. Why do you say that?"

"Quiet now. Can't you see I'm reading?"

"But Dad," I begged, trying not to sound sullen, "I'm having this tournament at school. I just have to have a paddle to play with, don't I?"

"You should have thought of that before."

"How could I have thought of it before? It was an accident. Can't I have a new one?"

"No!"

"Why not?"

"Because it's too expensive. If you want a new paddle, you will have to save your money. I won't pay for your clumsiness."

I was just about to finish the conversation in anger when my mother called. I turned and went into the kitchen.

"Listen, Jonas," she said calmly, "it'll be all right. Just wait and see."

"How?" I asked sulkily.

"There's a paddle or two up in the attic," she said, hugging me. "If you're lucky, they'll be good enough to play with. At least you can use them until you can get a new one."

"In the attic? Whose paddles?"

She reached out for the attic key hanging behind the kitchen door.

"They were Paul's," she said. "He was quite good. He and Daniel used to play. Daniel had a table in his basement."

"Has Daniel got a table-tennis table? I didn't know that."

"Well, he used to have one. I don't know if he still does. He wouldn't be able to use it now, would he?"

"Why not?"

She laughed, then looked at me in a questioning way.

"What's the matter with you, Jonas? Haven't you noticed that Daniel's been walking with a cane for the last two or three years?"

I blushed and shook my head.

"I just didn't think of it."

Daniel was one of my mother's childhood friends. He used to baby-sit for me when I was small. It had surprised me a lot when he began to walk with a cane. He was one year younger than my mother, and he looked even younger. And I was even more astonished when I heard of the reason for his disability. My father—who sometimes got tired of Daniel's closeness to me and my mother—told me the fine blood-vessels in Daniel's legs had been destroyed by too much alcohol, so that now he had to use a cane. "He's really a pitiful figure," my father said. And my mother—with her more humble approach to people in general, and Daniel in particular—couldn't explain it in any other way, although her words were different. It *was* the drinking that had ruined Daniel's legs, and forced him to use a cane years before he even turned fifty.

"I'll show you the paddles," Mother said. Then: "No, I can't. I'm going to see Else. It's almost three. You'll have to look for yourself. I believe they're in the wine-colored suitcase. I'll help you when I get back, if you can't find them."

I opened the door to the attic. I had never been there on my own before. I found the light switch and went in to the corridor of chicken-wire-clad cages.

Our cage was filled with skis, sleds, old lamps, clothes and bags. And an ugly dark-brown sideboard, behind which I could glimpse the wine-colored suitcase. I had to climb up on the sideboard to reach it.

The suitcase was big and heavy. With some effort I managed to lift it up on the sideboard before the attic light went off. After stumbling back to the switch, I opened the suitcase.

It was filled with clothes mostly, but there were also some books and two photo albums. I didn't recognize any of the things. They must have been Paul's, I thought. And I wondered why I hadn't been given them. I looked at a dark-gray pair of trousers, with a hardly visible checked pattern, and realized the clothes were all too big for me.

I searched for a moment before I found a table-tennis paddle. The rubber coating had dried out. It came loose from the wooden base as I ran my hand over it. Then I found the other paddle, and it seemed to be in better shape. I carefully smacked it against my knuckles. Yes, it seemed to be fine. Then the light went off again, and I turned it on. When I started to put the things back into the suitcase I saw a jacket lying at the bottom. It was a light-brown jacket, jeans-jacket style. I pulled it out and felt, to my surprise, that it was suede.

It was a bit stiff and smelled somewhat musty. And the right sleeve was damaged at the elbow. But it was just my size. I kept it on and put back the other things. I smiled as I walked to the stairs.

Mother was just about to leave as I entered the apartment. She froze when she saw me.

"Take that off immediately!" she cried.

"Why? What is it?"

"Take it off!"

Father heard us and came out to the hallway with the fishing magazine in his hand. He stopped abruptly when he saw me.

"Jesus!" he mumbled. And Mother had tears in her eyes.

"Take it off, Jonas," said my father, and put his arm around Mother.

"But it's just my size," I said. "It's so neat. You can't get jackets like this anymore. Can't you let me have it?"

Mother started to cry. Father looked at me and told me again to take off the jacket. I obeyed reluctantly. And Mother moved away from him and took the jacket from me. Tears were rolling down her cheeks.

"What's the matter?" I asked. "I know it's Paul's jacket, but I don't understand why you won't let me have it."

In an unaccustomed way, my father reached out and stroked my cheek. His hand was dry.

"It's the one he was wearing … when he died," he said in a low voice.

"Oh, look at me," Mother sobbed, wiping her eyes with the back of her hand. She put down the jacket and disappeared into the bathroom.

"Easy, Jonas," Father said. "We'll talk about this later. Right now we must let Mum get started or she'll be even more upset."

When Mother came out of the bathroom, she smiled at me, a bit embarrassed, and gently touched my cheek. Her hand smelled of soap.

"I have to leave now. Else is waiting. I'll be back in a couple of hours. Bye!"

The door closed. Father looked at me, not saying a word. And I realized suddenly that he looked like a little boy, sad and uncertain. He stroked the light-brown suede. Then he opened one of the wardrobe doors and squeezed the jacket in among the other clothes on the upper shelf. He really forced it in, as if the act was an effort.

I thought of Paul. And of my mother and father. And suddenly I felt all shaky and weak.

I went into my room and sat on the bed.

Paul's death was once again close. *Paul* was close.

I had seen the jacket he wore on the last of his forest walks. I had even tried it on. No wonder Mother was upset and sad when she saw me wearing it.

I thought of the damaged sleeve. Could it have been torn when Paul was hit by the train? Yes, that was probably the case. But it still didn't make sense. If he had worn the jacket when he was hit, shouldn't the jacket have been ripped to pieces? How is it that the person who wore the garment—my own brother—dies of his injuries, while the jacket gets away with a torn elbow? And how could he not avoid hearing the onrushing train? The engine must have been roaring, the rails must have been throbbing. Paul was standing right on the track. So I've been told by my mother and father.

Why didn't you throw yourself aside, Paul? What were you thinking of? What was it you saw in the forest that day?

I was lying on my bed, close to tears.

Suddenly I was aware of a soft humming sound coming from the living room. I got up and quietly opened my door.

It was Father. He was humming a tune.

I barely recognized the melody, but I had heard the words. I had heard the words several times before.

It's the time of the season, when your love runs high …

2

At times I'm surprised that I miss you. I've never met you. Still I miss you. As if I once knew you. As if I forgot you at some point, and now have started to think of you again. I used to dream about you. You would come to visit me, and it was always at night. And you told me things without actually speaking to me. I don't know how your voice sounded. In my dreams we have wordless conversations. And you—ever since I found it in the attic—always wear the light-brown suede jacket.

In the evening we sat talking in the living room. Mother, Father and me.

"You have to forgive me for yelling at you," Mother said, "but I had a shock when I saw you in his jacket. You're so … You're starting to look like him. What he looked like when he was fifteen."

"Did you think it was him?" I asked.

"No." Mother smiled. "You're not that much alike. And I don't really believe in ghosts. But still, it felt a bit like Paul was coming through the door. It wasn't *his* face, but you do look like him a great deal. I mean, it's obvious you're his brother. And you move like him. Sometimes your movements are just like his. And with the jacket on … his jacket, well …"

Father didn't speak. He was sitting next to Mother on the couch. He was absently looking out the window, his fingers tapping his thighs.

"Of course you can have the jacket if you want," Mother was saying. "You do need a new one, don't you? But perhaps we should take it to the dry cleaner's."

"It's a bit torn on one of the sleeves," I said. "Maybe we could fix it."

Mother was quiet for a while. I could see she was thinking of something. She raised her head, searching my father's face. He was still looking out the window. Then she made up her mind.

"Could you get the jacket for me?" she asked.

When I returned, Father looked away from the window and sat staring at the jacket on Mother's lap.

"Yes, I think we can fix it," Mother said, stroking the sleeve.

I wanted to say something, but I didn't dare. I was afraid I would make her sad again.

"That rip ... ?" I managed.

"Yes?"

"I mean, was that ... when he was hit?"

She shook her head. "I don't think he had the jacket on when it happened. I believe they said the jacket was found lying next to the track."

"But the rip?"

"That was earlier. I think he fell on his bike."

"Yes, I believe he did," Father said quietly.

"Try it on."

I hesitated.

"Try it on, Jonas," Mother repeated.

Slowly, I put it on.

"Yes, it's really nice," said Mother. "Daniel gave it to him when he turned thirteen. Or was it fourteen?"

She noticed my eyes were shining.

"Come," she said. "Come here, Jonas. You can sit here with us."

I sat down between my parents. And the tears came rolling.

"Hey, what's this?" Mother asked. "You shouldn't cry. It wasn't your fault I was upset."

"Yes, I know," I sobbed. "It's just … I have wanted so much to see him. You talk about him and tell me about him, but there is so much I will never know. I would have liked to be his younger brother for real. And he could have shown me the fox burrow and … and other things. He could have … we could have done so many things."

Mother was caressing my hair, Father carefully—a bit awkwardly—touching my leg.

"Yes, I know," said Mother, "but that's impossible. There must be thousands of people we all would have loved to meet, if only they were still alive. But we have to be satisfied being with those who live, those who are still alive. I too miss him very much. Even though I saw him every day for more than fifteen years, and even though he now has been dead almost as long as he lived, I still miss him so very much. Sometimes I feel like crying. It's as if … as if the grief gets weaker at times, it fades away, only to hit you again, even stronger. Like something living. And I'm always unprepared. And I'm absolutely attacked by grief, just as devastating as it ever was when it happened.

"You may think of Paul, or you may dream of him as much as you like, but you will never meet him. Unless there is a heaven, of course. In that case you will. And Stefan and I will see him too."

"You shouldn't be sorry," Father said gently. "You mustn't let the sorrow take over. If you do, it only gets worse."

"But I don't understand. Why didn't he jump aside? How could he miss hearing the train? I don't understand."

Mother took a deep breath. "Jonas, I don't understand it myself. And I've been thinking about it a lot. But Paul was a dreamer. He could sit for hours looking out the window without actually seeing anything. I guess he was dreaming. Or thinking of something. I had to call him several times before he even noticed me. I'm not sure, but maybe that's what happened. Maybe he just happened to be standing right there, on the track, when he thought of something, or dreamed of something, and so he didn't hear the train. I don't know, but it's all I can think of."

"But what did he dream of?"

"I don't know." Mother smiled. "Perhaps he was thinking of some girl he had met. What do you think?"

That night I dreamed about my brother.

Paul was sitting on my desk. He was wearing the light-brown suede jacket. By his side—hanging over the chair—was the same jacket, only now it was mine. Paul smiled when I looked at him. Behind him the window was black as coal.

"Hi, Jonas," he said.

"Hi, Paul."

"Are you dreaming of me?"

"Yes," I replied. "Quite often."

"Even now?" Paul asked.

"Yes, I think I am."

He laughed and leaned forward.

I sat up in my bed, my arms around my knees.

Paul took hold of the desk top, his hands next to his thighs. Then he leaned out even farther.

"Watch out!" I cried. "You might fall!"

He giggled.

"I don't fall," he said and fell toward the floor.

But he didn't fall. Instead, he stretched himself out, his hands almost reaching the ceiling. For a while he was absolutely still, calmly floating between the ceiling and the floor. Then, all of a sudden, he was next to my bed.

He bent over me and smiled.

"Little brother," he said.

I stretched out my hand to touch him, but as my fingers got near he was no longer there.

He was standing in front of the window.

"What were you dreaming of when you were standing on the railroad track?" I asked.

Paul turned and looked at me. Then he laughed and opened the window wide. A strong cold wind swept into the room and I pulled the blanket closer to my body.

"What were you dreaming of?" I screamed, trying to be heard over the roaring wind.

"Butterflies!" Paul yelled back.

And the open window was filled with silvery shining butterflies, sparklingly forcing themselves into my room. I tried in vain to catch a glimpse of my brother behind thousands and thousands of wings.

Then I woke up.

It was just as black outside my window as it had been in my dream. I could see the collar of his jacket, my jacket, hanging over the back of the chair. But Paul was gone.

I turned on my bed lamp, got up and fetched the jacket. It felt cold and stiff. After arranging the pillows, I took it with me to bed.

I held the jacket in front of me. I sniffed it. But all I could smell was the suede. Paul was no longer there.

I watched it carefully. The buttons were glowing in the lamp-light. A brass-colored shimmer. And I could feel the raised letters on one of the buttons: *Lee*. The seams were yellow. I followed them with my forefinger down the button strip and around the two breast pockets.

The pockets!

I opened the first one. There was something at the bottom. I pulled it out. It was an empty chewing gum wrapper of a sort I had never seen before. And there was actually still a sweet smell from the wrinkled paper.

I opened the second pocket. I could feel a tingle all through me when I realized there was a large piece of paper in it. The paper was folded, and I could see it had once been sealed with tape. The place where the tape had been had turned yellow. Carefully I unfolded it.

It was a letter. A letter written in a slightly sloping hand and with red ink.

Hi, Princi!
I never thought you'd answer my letter. I was really happy when I found your letter in the letterbox. My parents were watching me

reading it while we had breakfast. They were laughing and asking me if it was a love letter, but they didn't believe me when I told them. I was just smiling. The holiday will start on Saturday. Mum and Dad will go to the summerhouse, but I'll be home over the weekend. Alone! Why don't you come over? Ask your parents if you can stay with me over the night. Answer me soon. (Call me!) I want you to come. 'Cause I like you.
    P.S.

I turned over the paper but the other side was blank. I read it again. Who's Princi? And why were there no postscript and no sender? And why was a letter for Princi lying in my brother's jacket?

I put the letter in my treasure box and placed the jacket on the chair.

"Do you know anyone called Princi?" I asked my parents at breakfast.

"Princi? It must be a foreign name. Is it pronounced like that?"

"I'm not sure," I answered. "I just read it somewhere."

"Well, I've never heard it," said Mother. "Are you sure it's not an ordinary word? Prin … principal or something?"

"No," I said. "It has to be a name. I read it in a letter somewhere."

"Well, I don't know," said Mother, "but why don't you check at the library. I'm sure they have books on names, or some kind of encyclopedia."

"Yes, they probably have. But I would like to check it now, and they don't open until Monday."

"But you could call Daniel!" Mother exclaimed. "Or visit him. I know he'd be so glad. He often asks about you. You don't see each other very often these days."

Father looked annoyed. "Do you really think that's a good idea, his going to that man?" he asked in a low voice.

I could tell by her eyes she was angry.

"What do you mean?" she said. "Why is this not a good idea? Daniel is way too lonely. It would do him good if Jonas went to see him."

Father became sour and silent.

I waited quietly. I never understood why he was so worried about me. He had always been like that. Especially when I was to see Daniel. Perhaps he thought Daniel would offer me alcohol. I don't know.

"I think you should go." said Mother. "He would be so glad."

Daniel and Mother grew up on the same street, here in Oskarshamn, and they had known each other all their lives. When they were young, they were always together. They played together, they went to school together, they lived next to each other and they used to help each other with their homework, even though they were one grade apart. And when they grew older they used to spend their evenings at a small jazz club in town. By the way, that's where my mother and father first met.

Now, when I was fourteen, Daniel had a disability pension. Mother had told me he was a heavy drinker even when they were young, and this had escalated a year or so before I was born. He was drinking more or less daily. "But he always managed to do his job," Mother used to say. And Father would snort and protest: "Going to work with a hangover is not exactly like doing your job." And so the discussion would start.

It was only when Daniel began to have trouble walking that he was given the disability pension. And even though Father thought that this would make Daniel drink himself to death, he actually cut down on his drinking.

I knocked on Daniel's door.

"Come in!" he shouted.

His face beamed when he saw me. He had always been fond of me. But I thought I could see something else in his face as I stepped into his hallway, some kind of shadow that went as quickly as it came.

"Hello, Jonas," he said. "I'm glad you're here."

He got up from his chair and stumbled toward me. His hand tapped my shoulder, then gently touched my hair.

"Your hair is getting longer," he said, smiling.

He looked at my jacket.

"Do you recognize it?" I asked.

He nodded. "Yes, of course I recognize it. It was I who gave it to Paul. On his thirteenth birthday."

"Yes, I know. Father told me you said, 'Happy birthday, teenager,' when you gave it to him."

Daniel laughed. "Yes, I did. That's right. I had almost forgotten." He went silent for a moment. "You mean Stefan remembered? Well, you never know … Oh, we can't stand here. Come. Have a seat. Would you like some coffee?"

"Yes," I said, and sat down on the couch.

"Play a record, if you want to."

Daniel disappeared into his tiny kitchen.

I got up and started to look through his collection. Most of it was jazz records from the forties and fifties with artists I'd never heard of. It ended with my picking an album at random.

Daniel called from the kitchen: "Jonas, can you help me, please? I'm afraid I'm a little shaky ... "

Daniel smiled as he poured the coffee. "So, you're a Bill Evans fan."

"What?"

He laughed. "We're listening to him right now."

I giggled. "I didn't know. I just picked one."

We made small talk for a while. Then he asked if there was a particular reason for my visit.

"No, not exactly," I lied. "It's just, Mother told me you might have a book on names. One that tells you the meaning of a name and such. You see, I've found a name I've never heard before."

"Really? What name?"

"Princi."

At first he seemed unconcerned, slowly drawing on his cigarette. Then I saw how his hand suddenly shook, how he gave me a quick look before he glanced out the window. And then he repeated the name I had told him, but with a slightly different pronunciation.

"Where did you find it?" he asked.

"On a piece of paper I found. Or a letter, I guess."

"A letter," Daniel mumbled.

He went silent. The smoke from his cigarette spiraled up.

"Do you know this name?" I asked. "Have you heard it before?"

He looked at me. Nodded. "Yes. I know it. But it's not really a name."

"No?"

"No."

I waited for him to continue, but he was silent.

"What is it?"

"It's a word," he said, "just a word."

"A word? But, what does it mean?"

"It's a Czech word," said Daniel, "and it means *prince*."

"Prince?"

I don't remember if I was surprised at first and then happy, or if it was the other way around. I was surprised at the meaning of the word. It seemed so obvious once Daniel had told me. And I was happy. It meant someone who called my brother Prince could have written the letter. The letter could have belonged to my brother.

I saw Daniel was staring at me.

I looked down.

"Where did you find it?" he asked.

"In the attic," I said with some hesitation.

The piece on the record ended and a vibrant silence filled the room.

Daniel knew something about the letter, or at least he knew something of the one who was called Princi. And I felt caught. I shouldn't have told him where I read this strange name. But why was he so silent?

There was more music, this time a sad melody from a lonely piano. A few bars later it was followed by a soft drum and a bass.

"Well now, Jonas," Daniel began, "sometimes, when you're

sure you've forgotten, old memories just overwhelm you. You think you're safe. You think, what happened then doesn't matter anymore. But you're wrong, you're oh so wrong, 'cause sooner or later it will all come back. And you remember. And then the past is no longer far away. It's not even left or gone."

He went quiet, his face still. He looked out the window, through the room and out, without really looking at anything. Just like Paul in that school photograph, present but not present.

"Was Paul the one called Princi?" I asked.

Daniel nodded.

"Who called him Princi?"

Daniel suddenly bent forward and hid his face in his hands. For a short while I thought he would start to cry. I stared at him, terrified. But he straightened up and looked at me, sighing heavily. His eyes were red.

"Your brother Paul was one of the nicest persons I've ever met. God, I really liked him. And yet, after his death, he has become one of the most terrifying ghosts you can imagine. I'm not lying when I say I think of him every day."

"What do you mean, one of the most terrifying ghosts you can imagine?"

Daniel chuckled. "Well, I guess you could call it silly, my using that expression. Of course, I don't mean Paul is visiting me with a white sheet wrapped around him. No. But he's visiting my dreams, my nightmares. Perhaps I shouldn't tell you this, I don't know, but, you see, it's as if he is blaming me for what happened, as if it's my fault. And I always try to make him explain why I'm the guilty one, but he never does. He just looks at me with those beautiful eyes ..."

"But why should you be guilty of Paul's death?" I asked. "I don't understand that. He was hit by the train because he was thinking of something else—a girl or something ..."

Daniel sighed and looked at me. "No, Jonas. That's not what I mean. That's not what he's blaming me for."

"Then, what is it?"

He shook his head. "I can't tell you. Not now."

"But who was it that called him Princi? You could at least tell me that."

"No, actually, I can't, because I don't know."

"But I thought you—"

"I don't know, Jonas," he interrupted. "Paul was here one day—a couple of months before he died—and he was so happy. Exhilarated." He stopped and glanced at the bookshelves. "I actually took a picture of him that day. I'll show you."

He got up slowly and went over to one of the shelves.

"Let's see," he mumbled, and started to look through a photo album. "Yes. That's it. Here it is."

And it was you, Paul. You are sitting in a chair in front of the window. You are wearing the suede jacket. Your arms are crossed over your stomach. I can clearly see the rip on the right sleeve. And you are smiling. You are smiling and your eyes are shining. I have never seen you so happy. Your eyes are shining and you are looking straight into the camera.

"He looks so happy," I said.

"Yes, he was really happy that day. That's why I wanted to take the picture. You see, he wasn't always happy, your brother. He often felt sad, and lonely."

"Lonely? But he had lots of friends. And everybody liked him."

"Yes, that's right. But still, he often felt lonely and sad. You can do that even if you have friends, can't you?"

"Well, maybe."

I looked again at the picture.

"Can you see?" Daniel said in a low voice. "Can you see how beautiful he was? He had such lovely eyes, and when he smiled ..."

"What?"

"Well, he had a contagious smile. Everyone was warmed by it, and by his laughter."

"Like when you're in love."

Daniel looked at me.

"Yes," he said slowly, "like when you're in love."

"But why was he so happy that day?"

"Well, you see, someone had fallen for that smile, for those eyes. Someone else. That's what he told me that day. That's why he came. He wanted to tell me he was in love. That he had met somebody. That's why he was so happy."

"Tell me more."

"Well, he didn't tell me anything else. He just told me he had fallen in love. I don't know where or how they met. But I remember his saying that they would go to see the bonfires on Walpurgis Night. Paul had even bought some fireworks, though I guess Sara must have forbidden him. She was always so afraid he'd be hurt."

"I know. She's always like that. But who was it he had met? What was her name?"

It was a while before Daniel answered.

"I don't know who he had met. I don't remember his mentioning a name. But he told me his new acquaintance called him

Princi. He smiled when he told me that, and said it was the Czech word for prince. I remember thinking the name suited him."

"But didn't you ask who he had met?"

"No, I didn't. But I asked Paul what *he* called the one *he* had fallen in love with."

"What did he say?"

Daniel smiled. "He didn't say a thing. He just smiled and did this."

And Daniel put his forefinger over my lips. "Hush!"

"What did he mean by that?"

"I don't know. I guess he didn't want to tell me."

Daniel started going through the photo album. Here and there he pointed at a picture and told me a thing or two about it. One of the pages was different from the others. A black line framed four pictures. They were pictures from my brother's funeral. I could see the white coffin in all of them.

Mother and Father were there, though I really saw just my father. The woman by his side—Mother—was wearing a black veil over her face.

I tried to find someone else, someone I didn't know.

"Do you think she's in these pictures?" I asked.

"Who?"

"The girl Paul was in love with."

Daniel shook his head. "No, Jonas. The one he was in love with was not at the funeral."

"No? How come? Were they not lovers anymore?"

Daniel didn't answer. Instead, he bent forward and reached for a cigarette. While he lit it I repeated my questions.

"Was it like that? Were they not lovers? Maybe they didn't like each other anymore."

"You ask a lot of questions."

"But I want to know," I said, while trying to fan away the cigarette smoke. "Why don't you tell me?"

Daniel laughed quietly. "Well, I don't want to sound secretive, but sometimes it might be best not to tell the whole story. At least not at once. I've told you quite enough already. Perhaps I can tell you more some other time. In time. If you're still interested ..."

"But can't you—"

"No, not now."

"But I would like to—"

Daniel sighed. "Please, Jonas, I don't want to tell you any more for the moment. That you will have to accept."

"Okay," I answered sulkily, "but I *would* like to know. I wish I had my own memories of Paul, and all that happened to him, but I don't. That's why I have to ask the ones who knew him, the ones who met him." I stopped and looked at Daniel. "Please, couldn't you tell me a little more?"

But Daniel came close and silenced my lips with his forefinger.

"Hush!"

3

There was a note lying on the kitchen table when I got home.

Hi, Jonas!
   We've gone shopping. Also thinking of visiting Grandma and Grandpa for a while. We'll be home by eight. There's a pan with soup in the fridge. Warm it up if you're hungry.
   Mum

I looked at the clock. A quarter past five. No, I wasn't hungry.
   I fetched the attic key.
   The wine-colored suitcase was standing where I had left it, right inside the door. I was filled with an almost devout feeling. I picked up the gray-checked trousers and the other clothes and put them on top of the sideboard.
   When the light went off I lit my flashlight. And so I picked out Paul's books. I recognized some of the titles. I had borrowed them myself from the library. I put aside those I hadn't read.
   Then I took out the first photo album. There was writing on the inside of the binder: *This photo album belongs to Paul Lund-*

berg. 6 November 1967. I recognized the handwriting. It belonged to my mother.

The first pages were filled with school photographs. With the flashlight I examined the black-and-white pictures in the search for my brother. He was smiling in the picture from his first year at school. In all the others his face was serious. I couldn't find any photograph from Paul's fifth grade. But beside the picture from his sixth grade was a copy of the photograph that stood on the TV set.

I turned the pages. In some pictures I found Daniel. In the first one he was standing on a beach, laughing. He looked so young. In the next picture he himself was holding a camera, pointing it toward the photographer.

Then there were some pictures of Paul I had never seen before. In the first one he was sitting alone on a rock by the shore. He was wearing a pair of checked swimming trunks. A large towel was hanging over his shoulders. He was smiling at the camera.

In the second picture Daniel had joined him. They were sitting close together on the rock. Daniel was laughing, Paul was smiling broadly, and Daniel's arm rested on my brother's shoulder.

The other pictures I recognized from the album belonging to my mother and father. Birthdays and Christmases. I studied carefully the pictures from Paul's thirteenth birthday. Yes, there was the light-brown suede jacket in one picture of Mother and Paul that had been taken in the kitchen. I could see it, lying on the table behind my mother and my brother. Beside it was an ashtray. A thin bit of smoke from a glowing cigarette was spiraling up. It must be Daniel's.

I brought the album close and studied Paul's face. He seemed to be so happy. And I could see we were alike. I could clearly see the likeness. Almost like brothers.

Then I opened the other album. Once again Mother had written Paul's name on the inside of the binder. And a date: *28 December 1968.* Perhaps the album was a delayed Christmas gift.

The first photograph was of my parents. Our parents. They were standing arm in arm outside the garage on the other side of the yard. They were laughing and looking into the camera. Father had long sideburns. And on the right side of my mother and my father there was a glimpse of an old dusty Volvo.

Then I turned the page.

A picture of a boy I didn't recognize filled the page. It was taken outdoors. In the background I could see snow and something that looked like an outhouse. The boy could be fourteen or fifteen. He had straight black hair. He was smiling. He was wearing a dark heavy coat, which appeared to be rather ragged. The upper buttons were undone. The unbuttoned part revealed a neck that looked far too naked in the wintry environment. Still, he didn't seem to be cold. He was smiling, and his glittering dark eyes were turned toward the photographer. You're so beautiful, I thought. And read the text beside the picture: *Down by the bay. March 1969. Petr je tady.*

"Petr je tady?" I whispered. "What does it mean?"

The next page had four black-and-white pictures. The first one was of you, Paul. It was taken in my room. Or your room, rather. You're standing in front of the desk, leaning with one hand on the back of the chair. Whoever took the photo must have been in the doorway to the hall. You're looking at the photographer. Your eyes and your lips are playfully showing that secret smile you sometimes have in the picture on top of the television. You're holding a notebook in your other hand. It looks like the notebooks we used in school in the first grades, only this one is thicker.

In the second picture you're nude, moving out from a bathroom as someone catches you with the camera. Your hair is wet and straggly. In your right hand you're holding what I think is a towel. The picture is a bit blurred right there, since you were moving your hand. Perhaps you were trying to cover yourself in front of the photographer. You would look like a little boy, if it weren't for the dark hair above your crotch.

The third picture is a nature scene, a rock by the sea. Waves are crashing against the rock. A lone pine tree bends in the wind. The sky shows thunderclouds.

And then—in the fourth picture—the boy from the winter picture is back. He is squatting on top of the rock. The wind ruffles his hair. He's looking toward the sea and the waves. There is a shoulder bag by his side, and he is holding its strap.

There was no text to any of the pictures. Still, I could feel strongly that they were connected. There was a common thread, which I—at this point—could only sense.

I decided to return to the apartment. I wanted to be there when my mother and father came home.

They had not returned. The clock in the kitchen showed twenty minutes to seven.

I went into my room and put the books on my desk. Then I stood holding the photo albums in my hands, wondering where to hide them. That's right, hide them. Because it felt as if I were poking into something I wasn't supposed to, and I didn't want my mother and father to know about it.

I put the albums in the bottom of my wardrobe. Before I covered them with the old clothes and stuff that normally lies there, I took another look at the picture of Paul on his way out of the bathroom.

There was something strange about that photo. I had a tingling sensation in my stomach. I could see we resembled each other. And I felt I wanted to touch him, touch his body. Or mine.

That evening I was lying in bed thinking of the things Daniel had told me. I understood he must know at least some of the answers to my questions. But I couldn't understand why he didn't want to tell me the whole story.

Before I had gone to bed I had a talk with my mother in the kitchen.

"I went to see Daniel today," I told her.

"So you did go," she said. "That's good. Could he help you?"

"With what?"

She laughed. "With that name, of course. Princi, or whatever it was."

"Oh, yes, he could. But it's no name. It's just like you said. It's just a word. Even though someone seems to have used it as a nickname."

"What are you up to?" she asked.

"What do you mean?"

"You're up to something. That I can tell. You look like you do when you're solving a crossword or playing chess. I could see it when we got home. What is it you're trying to solve? Can I help in any way?"

I hesitated. "I'm not sure. Maybe."

Mother smiled. "Maybe, you say. Maybe I can help. In what way?"

"I'm not really sure," I repeated. "Perhaps by just talking to me."

"Talking to you? But we talk all the time. Even now. Well, anyway, what do you want to know?"

"Well, yesterday when we were talking about Paul, you said he might have been thinking of a girl he had met. Do you know who that girl was?"

Mother shook her head. "No. I don't even know if he had met a girl."

"But you said you thought he was thinking of a girl, didn't you?"

"I don't know what he was thinking of. It was just something I said. Paul never said anything about a girl. Someone special, I mean. Not as far as I can remember. I don't know what he was thinking of. I meant it as a suggestion. *Perhaps* he was thinking of a girl, perhaps it was something else. I don't know."

"Was he like that often? Daydreaming, I mean?"

"Yes, I guess you could say that." She paused. "Stefan and Paul were a lot alike in that way. And you know how Dad is. Yes, it happened quite often."

"Do you think he was sad?" I asked. "Could that have been the reason he was dreaming?"

"Sad? No, I don't think he was sad. Why do you ask that? He wasn't a sad kind of person. Not sadder than you or me."

I turned away. "Daniel said Paul was sad now and then."

"Daniel," she whispered. "Well … Yes, perhaps he was, but at home he was happy most of the time. And we talked a lot, Paul and I. About everything. But when he visited Daniel … well …"

"Yes?"

Mother sighed. "Well, I don't know. Perhaps you've noticed it yourself. I mean, Daniel isn't exactly a happy kind of person. I mean, he's often feeling low. At times even depressed. And Paul spent a lot of his time with Daniel. Perhaps it was easier for Paul to talk about things that made him sad, when he was at Daniel's place. I mean, it might have been that … that atmosphere at Daniel's … An atmosphere that made it easier to talk about sorrow and sad thoughts."

"Was Daniel feeling low even when you were young?" I asked.

"Daniel has always been a bit low-spirited. It's in his nature, I suppose. But I've always liked him. A lot."

"But why is he sad?"

She shook her head. "Well, Jonas, you'll have to ask Daniel about that if you really want to know. I don't want to talk about his feelings. It would be like gossiping, don't you think?"

"Yeah."

We sat in silence. From the living room we could hear the theme from some TV series. I looked out the kitchen window, and suddenly remembered my dream.

"Was Paul interested in butterflies?"

Mother laughed. "Oh, Jonas, you never stop confusing me. What makes you think that?"

I smiled, a bit embarrassed. "It was something I dreamed, that's all."

She reached out and touched my cheek.

"You're sweet," she said, "but I'm sorry to say, I don't think he was especially interested in butterflies. I mean, he was interested in almost everything in nature: mammals, trees, birds, creepy insects, and whales. And probably also butterflies. What did you dream?"

"I dreamed Paul was in my room. And I asked him, in my dream, what *he* dreamed of. And he told me he dreamed about butterflies. That's it. Then I woke up. No … Not really. Then the window suddenly opened and thousands of butterflies flew into my room …"

Mother smiled. "A beautiful dream."

"What was it that made Paul sad?"

"I don't know."

"You never saw him sad?"

"Of course I did. But that only happened every now and then. Nothing constant. Or not at all. But, yes, I saw him sad."

Then she suddenly thought of something. "Yes, that's right. Paul was sad that last night. I just remembered. Strange. I had almost forgotten."

"What? Why was he sad?"

"He had a nightmare," she told me. "His crying woke me up. So I went to his room. And I noticed he was crying in his sleep. He wasn't awake. And I sat down by his side and whispered something to comfort him. His name, I guess. And he woke up. Oh, he was so sad. Like an abandoned child. I asked why he cried. And he said, 'I had a terrible dream.' I remember I wiped away his tears while I asked him what he had dreamed."

I bent closer and held Mother's hand.

"What did he say?"

"He said, 'I dreamed my castle was burning down.' That's right, that was what he said. 'I dreamed my castle was burning down and everyone inside was killed.'"

Mother started to cry.

I held her hand and whispered, "Easy, now. Easy." And the lines in her face were blurred by my own tears.

Father came into the kitchen.

"What is it, darling?" he asked, as he squatted by her side.

"Oh, it's nothing," she sobbed. "I was just thinking of Paul. And so I became ... Oh, it's nothing."

Father sighed, then glared at me. "Do you have to talk about him?" he asked.

"We were just—" I started, but Mother interrupted.

"No, we don't. I was just thinking of Paul's last night. Do you remember? He had a nightmare that night ..."

Father nodded and took her hand. "Yes, of course I remember."

"I had almost forgotten," Mother said, drying her tears. "And so, quite suddenly, something made me remember. That's strange. Perhaps it was because Jonas told me about his dream. Well, I'm all right now."

"Are you sure?" asked Father.

Mother smiled. "Yes, I am. I'm fine now, thank you."

4

A few weeks later I dreamed of you again.

I was walking through a landscape of strange, somber colors. And even though I didn't recognize myself I knew the road would lead me up to a house I still couldn't see, a house I had never visited before. And then, all of a sudden, I was there. The house was very large and gray, but the windows shone with all the colors of the rainbow. Like the windows of some south-European cathedral.

I knocked on the door.

Paul opened it. He smiled.

"Hello, Jonas. I'm painting. Why don't you come in."

I followed him up wide stairs and down a long hallway.

Paul opened a pair of doors at the end of the hallway. We entered a large room. The windows were incredibly high. I could barely see the vaulting.

The room was almost empty. But in one corner a naked boy was perched on a stool. In front of him was an easel.

"Come!" Paul said and took my hand.

We went up to the easel. Paul pointed at the painting.

"Do you like it?" he asked.

I looked at the painting. But the colors were not still. And the strokes of the brush seemed to be moving over the canvas, as if they couldn't make up their minds. The lines were constantly shifting, the colors constantly changing.

"I'm not sure," I answered.

The naked boy had come down from his stool and was standing beside my brother. His eyes were dark and strange.

He turned and stood in front of my brother. He reached out his arms. With his hands he felt Paul's hair, forehead, eyes and nose. His fingers followed the outline of Paul's lips. Then he lowered his arms, caressed Paul's chest, Paul's hips. Paul was laughing.

The boy continued to feel his way over Paul's body. His dark eyes were wide open, yet he didn't seem to be focusing on anything.

"I see," I said.

Paul looked at me. "What is it you see?" he asked.

"That boy is trying to get a picture of you by using his hands. He has to use his hands because he can't see. He's blind."

Paul laughed. The other boy was also laughing.

"No, Jonas," Paul said. "You're wrong. He's not blind at all. You're the one who's blind. You're the one who can't see."

And so everything went black, and I woke.

"What a strange dream," I whispered to myself.

I got up from my bed and carefully opened the wardrobe door. Just as carefully I took out one of the photo albums and returned to bed.

I was looking at the pictures of that other boy, the one someone—probably my brother—had taken pictures of down by the bay the year before I was born. I examined them closely. Yes, it was the dark eyes of the boy in my dream. It was the same boy.

But in the pictures he seemed to be seeing. Was it really like Paul had said, that I was the one who couldn't see? That I was the blind one?

If so, what was it that I couldn't see?

The painting!

That's it. I hadn't seen the painting. But, no, it didn't make sense. I *did* see the painting, although the lines and colors never made a complete picture. Paul's painting wasn't showing itself to me. Or perhaps the motif was there all the time, only I was blind.

I looked for clues in the photographs, but I was way too tired. Thoughts were tumbling in my head. My eyes constantly returned to the dark eyes of that other boy, and to my brother.

The photo album slipped out of my hands as I fell asleep.

5

During the following eighteen months I often thought of you, of what I had dreamed and what I had been told. Often I looked in the photo albums, but I still couldn't understand what it was I didn't see, although I realized my not seeing actually had nothing to do with the painting in my dream.

A couple of times I tried to persuade Daniel to tell me his secrets, but he still didn't want to. So, I continued my search for clues among your photographs.

It was early in the evening a couple of days before my sixteenth birthday. I was lying in bed reading when the phone rang. Mother answered. She talked for a while, but I couldn't hear what she said. Then she called.

"It's Daniel. He wants to talk with you."

"Hi, Jonas, it's me," Daniel said. "I hope I'm not interrupting anything."

"No, not at all."

"You see, I won't be here for your birthday. I'll be visiting my brother. So I thought you could come over tonight, if you want. I have a small present for you."

"Yes, of course," I said. "I'd like to come."

I closed the door to my room and opened the wardrobe door. I took out my treasure box and the two photo albums. Some of the pictures had been glued to the pages, something I had already noticed the first time I looked at them, but the rest were attached with photo mounts. Carefully I removed the two pictures of that other boy, plus two of the pictures of Paul.

Then I saw something. Someone had written on the back of one of the photographs of the other boy: *Mému malému Princi.*

I stared at the strange words, before once again hiding the albums and the treasure box.

"Well, Jonas," Daniel said after we had eaten, "I guess it's time for your present."

He smiled and rose from his chair to fetch a small red package.

"You'll have to excuse the Christmas paper. It was all I had. Here you go!"

"Thanks!"

I sat looking at the packet in my hands.

"Come on, now! You don't have to wait for your birthday."

I ripped off the tape and the paper—Christmas red and gold—and found two small boxes.

"Open them," Daniel urged.

In the first box there was a small, carved wooden figure, an ebony-black creature with large eyes.

"It looks a bit like that Klee figure on the wall," Daniel said, "but it's from Africa. From Ghana. They call it *Akua ba*. The goddess of fertility, or love, if you prefer. You can wear it round your neck, or put it on your wall."

"It's very nice. Thanks, Daniel!"

He smiled and pointed at the second box.

I opened it, and found some rolled-up banknotes.

"It's better you buy what you want."

"You're crazy," I said. "This is too much."

"No, it's not."

"Thank you!" I repeated.

We sat in silence for a while, listening to music, sipping our coffee. I was looking through a book on art. Then I remembered my envelope. I went out to the hallway to get it.

"What's that you've brought?" Daniel asked. "Is it a letter?"

I nodded.

"Is it … is it *the* letter? The one you found in the attic?" He gave me a searching look. "Why did you bring it?"

"I wanted to show it to you. I thought, perhaps you wanted to …"

He sighed and shook his head. "You never give up, do you? What are you up to? Sara told me you're questioning her as well. Even though she doesn't seem to mind. Quite the opposite. She thinks it's exciting. But I'm not sure … Where will it lead you? I've told you before, I don't want to be secretive, but I'm not sure your questions are going to lead to anything good. What do you want? What are you hoping to find?"

"My brother," I answered quietly.

Daniel was silent for a moment.

"What you're asking about, Jonas, is a delicate matter. I'm not sure you'll like what you find. Perhaps you will even hate it. Or some of the persons involved."

"Hate?" I was surprised. "I won't hate anyone. Why should I? All I want is to get to know my brother. I want to *know* him. Who he was, I mean."

Daniel was quiet for a while. Then he began to speak.

"I can very well understand why you want to learn about your brother, I really do. You're a bit of a romantic, I guess, and you want to get an image of your dead brother. You want him to be closer. I can understand that, Jonas, and I would probably do the same if I were you. Though I'd probably hesitate before asking some of those questions. But then again, why should you even think there would be …

"Searching into the past can be like turning a stone. Most of the time you find nothing but disgusting, creepy things." He stopped and looked at me. "What I'm saying is, during your search you may find unpleasant things you'd wish you'd never found."

He paused and lit a cigarette.

"All right, Jonas. It's a deal. You can ask whatever you want. But I'm not promising to answer all your questions. Is that okay with you?"

I didn't know where to start, so I took out the letter and gave it to him.

He looked at it, slowly reading.

"Strange handwriting," he murmured.

"Yes, that's what I thought when I saw it. When I first read it, I mean. But now I believe the letter was written by someone who learned to write in another country. That's why we think the handwriting is a bit strange. I believe it's written by someone who was born in Czechoslovakia."

"Yes?"

"That is just a guess, of course, but since *Princi* is Czech, and the handwriting in the letter is different …"

I was watching Daniel while I spoke. His face revealed nothing.

"What do you think?" I asked.

"It could be like that."

"You're the one who told me what Princi meant. You're the one who said it was Czech. But then, when you did, I didn't think of asking how you knew."

"Well, I didn't know until Paul told me," said Daniel.

"That's it. That's what I thought. But *what* did he tell you? Did he just say it was Czech? Didn't he say anything about the one who taught him the word?"

"Not much."

"But something?"

He hesitated. "Well, he said that the one who called him Princi came from Czechoslovakia."

I smiled.

Daniel looked at me, puzzled.

"You did it again," I said.

He threw out his arms. "What?"

"You said …"

"Yes?"

I took a deep breath. "When you told me someone had fallen in love with Paul, I asked if you knew her name. But you didn't. You said you couldn't remember any name. And when I asked you if she was at the funeral, you said, 'The one he was in love with was not at the funeral.' And now, just now you said, 'The one who called him Princi' came from Czechoslovakia."

I barely dared to continue.

Daniel's eyes were fixed on me. "Yes?" he said. "And?"

"I think … I believe the one who was in love with Paul was a boy. A Czech boy."

All was quiet. The air was fragile. I barely dared breathe.

Daniel was pale. He drew on his cigarette, and didn't look at me.

"That's how it was, isn't it?"

"Yes."

I sighed with relief.

Daniel got up and started to walk round the room, stiffly and stumblingly. Now and then he stopped, looked at something, touched something. For a while he stood before the bookshelves looking at a picture I recognized from my mother's photo album: a childhood picture of Daniel and Mother and a large Russian wolfhound named Dourak. I still remember the first time she told me the dog's name. I thought it sounded like something out of a fairy tale, magical.

Daniel turned and we looked at each other.

"Yes, that's how it was," he began, but his voice was not the same. "It was a boy. And he did come from Czechoslovakia. But I don't remember what he was called. Paul mentioned his name, but I don't really remember it. I only know it started with an M." Then he looked at me. "Jonas," he said softly, "how on earth did you know?"

I shrugged. "I just had a feeling …"

"But I was the only one who knew," said Daniel. "I was the only one he told, the only one he dared to tell. Sara didn't know, she still doesn't. Nor Stefan. I was the only one who knew."

"When did Paul tell you about it?" I asked. "That he was … I mean …"

Daniel nodded. "I remember it well. I even remember the date, because it was the night before the Lucia celebrations. The twelfth of December, 1968."

"At night?"

"Yes. At night."

"Tell me."

Daniel asked me to get a beer from the fridge.

I poured it into a large glass and put it in front of him.

"Thanks. Have a Coke or something, if you want."

I shook my head. "No, I'm fine. Now, tell me about Paul. Tell me what happened the night before the Lucia celebrations."

6

"**It was** the night before Lucia," Daniel began. "I remember it well. I was here, at home, listening to the radio. It was a memorial program on Jan Johansson. Perhaps you've heard of him. He was a jazz pianist. He had been killed a few days earlier in a traffic accident. They were playing his music and talking about him, and during one of the pieces, I heard a knock on my door. At first I thought it was someone who wanted to complain about my radio being too loud. It was already half-past eleven. So I turned down the volume. And just as I got to the door, I heard someone crying on the other side. When I opened it, Paul fell into the hall, into my arms. Tears were rolling down his cheeks. He smelled of alcohol. I led him inside, helped him take off his boots and his jacket.

"He leaned against me as we sat down on the couch. And he cried even more. 'Easy now, easy,' I said, trying to comfort him. And I held him close. He seemed so small in my arms, though he was almost as big as I was. And he cried for a long time ...'"

I waited—quietly—for Daniel to continue.

"When he stopped crying, I asked if he wanted something to drink. He had been walking all the way from town, and it was cold outside. He nodded and said he'd like to have some hot chocolate, so I made him a cup. Then I sat down close by his side and asked him what had happened. And so he told me he was more interested in boys than girls, that he had known about it for several years, but that he, all the time, or at least at the beginning, had tried to crush it. He thought the toughest part was in the gym at school, where he could see all the other boys in his class in the locker room and in the showers. And he tried not to look. But it was difficult.

"He told me there was a boy in his parallel-class who had interested him for a long time. I believe he was called Göran. Yes, that's it, Göran. And Paul told me Göran too was looking at the other boys. Göran used to pretend that the other boys 'were girls,' and he pawed them in the showers, laughing all the time. Göran was much bigger and stronger than the others, so no one dared stop him.

"I didn't say a word, at least not at the start. But then Paul became silent. He was just sitting here by my side, warming his hands with his cup of hot chocolate. And I asked him if something special had happened that evening. He nodded. 'Tell me,' I begged. 'Perhaps that will help you.' And, for the first time that evening, he smiled."

Daniel was rubbing his eyes. "Can you imagine that, Jonas? He smiled, even though he was so shaken."

"Did he tell you what had happened?" I asked, feeling close to tears.

"Yes, he did. He told me he had been invited to a party, a Lucia party. Some friends of one of his classmates were having the party in town. Without any parental supervision. Paul went there with a couple of friends. They were drinking. I don't think they drank that much, but I guess they weren't used to it. Paul got rather drunk, and that helped him try to get closer to Göran.

"Paul was standing in the hallway, queuing for the bathroom, when Göran came up behind him. They started to talk, and Paul suddenly got dizzy from the alcohol. He told me he would have fallen if Göran hadn't grabbed him. Only Göran didn't let go, even when Paul regained his balance. He was standing close to Paul, holding him. And so Paul kissed him. Göran laughed and asked if Paul had a crush on him. 'Maybe,' Paul said. Göran laughed. 'So you're gay?' But Paul didn't think it was a derisive laugh and repeated his 'Maybe.'

"Then the bathroom was empty. And Paul asked Göran if he wanted to go in with him. Göran wondered why. 'We could cross-pee,' said Paul.

"Göran followed him. It was he who locked the door. And when they were done, Göran turned and asked Paul if he really had meant what he'd said in the hallway. 'Of course,' Paul said. Göran came close, gripped Paul's hand, stopped him from closing his fly. 'What are you doing?' Paul asked. 'Touching you,' Göran answered, and started to … started to rub his crotch. Paul was all confused. He told me he had been both excited and scared at the same time. 'Here,' Göran said, pulling Paul's hand to his genitals."

I was listening intently to Daniel's story. I pulled my legs up on the couch and sat holding my knees.

"Are you cold?" Daniel asked. "Do you want me to close the window?"

"No, I'm not cold. I'm fine."

"Well, he told me he felt Göran's penis harden in his hand. Still he didn't dare do what Göran asked him to. 'So you're a coward!' Göran said. And Paul replied that he wanted them to go somewhere else. 'There's a queue outside. They all want to use the bathroom.' Göran was irritated. 'You wanted me to come in with you,' he snapped. 'You could at least *do* something.' But Paul said he didn't want to. And he stepped back.

"Göran closed his fly and pushed Paul hard in the chest. Since he was totally unprepared, Paul lost his balance and fell, hitting his head on the tub. He didn't have time to get up before Göran opened the door. One of the queuers was standing there. 'What's going on?' he asked. And Paul could hear Göran answer from outside in the hall, 'It's that bloody queer, Paul. He was trying to grope me at the toilet.'

"Paul heard the laughter from the others. He got up, closed his fly, and went past the boy in the doorway. He came out in the hall in time to hear another classmate say, 'But, Göran, what were you doing in there with another guy in the first place?' And Paul saw Göran hit the other boy in the face. The boy fell to the floor, and blood sprang from his nose. He started to cry. 'What the fuck!' Göran screamed. 'Are you crying? Maybe you're queer too!'

"Paul got his jacket and rushed out and home, to me."

"What a bastard!" I burst out. "How could Göran do something like that?"

Daniel shook his head. "Don't judge people so quickly. Göran was probably as scared as Paul. They were only reacting in different ways. Göran got mad and used his fists, while Paul preferred to get away."

"I still think Göran acted like a swine," I grumbled. "You can't behave like that."

Daniel leaned close and touched my hand.

"Yes, Jonas, you can. People do it all the time. They hurt each other, torment each other. Only because they themselves are uncertain or incapable of understanding, or are unwilling to understand. It happens all the time. And I did warn you, didn't I? I said the things I would tell you wouldn't all be pleasant."

I nodded. A moment later I asked Daniel to continue.

"That's enough for now. It's getting late. And Sara doesn't want you to be too late."

"I know."

I still hadn't shown Daniel the photographs I had brought. And I hadn't learned anything about the Czech boy who called my brother Princi. And there was also something else I wanted to ask Daniel about.

"Just a little more," I begged.

He shook his head.

"No, that's enough. I can tell you more another day, perhaps. At least, now you know a little more. Oh, by the way, don't mention this to Sara or Stefan, will you? They don't know. And there's no reason why they should. I mean, it would only upset them. And, I don't want that. If Paul hadn't died when he was young, it would have been only a matter of time before they knew he was gay. I mean, they would have heard about it in a more … well, in a more usual way. But since he died before he could tell them himself … Well, anyway, they don't have to know about it now. It would only upset them. I wouldn't have told you, but you had figured it out yourself. Whatever made you do that? I don't understand … But promise me you won't tell your parents about this."

"Of course," I said, "but you must promise to tell me more some other day."

Daniel frowned. "That's blackmail."

"I'm sorry, I didn't mean it like that. I just want you to tell me more. Can you do that? And I have things to tell *you* ..."

Daniel laughed.

"Yes, I believe you have. Well, we'll see ..."

Daniel was standing in the doorway, watching me put on the suede jacket.

"It's nice, that jacket," he said. "It suits you."

"Yes, so Mother and Father tell me. It's getting to be a bit small, though."

I tied my shoelaces, stood up, and looked at Daniel. I wanted to go to him, but he seemed so faraway. I took one step. "You know, Daniel—"

I was stopped by a phone call.

"It's probably Sara," Daniel said, "wanting to know if you're still here. Run along now, so I don't have to lie to her."

"But ..."

He came up to me, put one hand on my shoulder and lightly touched my cheek with the other.

"Run along now, Jonas. We'll meet soon."

7

The spring term had started, but I was home in bed with the flu. When the fever fell, I began to feel really bored. So I took out Paul's photo albums.

I was lying in bed looking at the picture where you come out from some bathroom. I tried to see your eyes, but the image wasn't sharp enough. For a while I even believed I could see the mark of Göran's hand on your chest. Like some kind of stigmatization. But that was probably just my imagination. And I tried to see the likeness everyone said we had, though I didn't think we were that much alike.

Then I came to think of the long mirror on the inside of one of the wardrobe doors in the hallway.

I got up from the bed and opened the wardrobe. Yes, I could see my reflection from the bathroom doorway. But there was something missing. That's it! The towel! I took a towel from its hook, held it in my right hand, and posed in the same way you were standing in the photo. Yes, now we were more alike. But there was still something that was different. It was my hair. Your hair was wet and straggly. I hesitated for a moment, then wet my hair at the sink.

For a long time I just stood there, looking at your picture, taken outside another bathroom some seventeen years earlier, and the reflection of me. We were really alike. Even though I was a bit thinner. But we were alike. Just like brothers.

And right then Father opened the door at the other end of the hallway.

"Hello!" he called.

I rapidly closed the bathroom door and locked it.

"Hi, Dad!" I shouted, and started to dry my hair.

I could hear him close the wardrobe door. And realized I had left my underpants in my room.

I checked my hair. It was almost dry. Then I flushed the toilet.

Father was sitting by the kitchen table with the newspaper. He looked up when I opened the bathroom door. Our eyes met. Here we go, I thought.

"For God's sake, Jonas!" he burst out. "You shouldn't be running around naked when you're sick. You'll never get better."

"Yes, I know. But I had to rush to the toilet."

I quickly disappeared into my room, and hid the photograph. Then I dressed and went out to Father, who asked: "Are you still feverish?"

"No, I don't think so. But my head and my chest are still aching." And I coughed a bit.

He closed his newspaper and scratched his shoulder.

"Have you been in bed all day?"

I nodded.

"You're bored, aren't you?"

"I am."

"You could read."

"Yes, I guess. But I don't really feel like it."

"Then you'll have to think of something else to do," he said.

"Something you can do in bed. 'Cause I think you should stay in bed a little longer. You could sketch. I used to sketch when I was young and unwell. Or you could write. Don't look so surprised. You could write a letter, for instance. To a friend. Or to Grandma. Or you could write a diary. Just like Paul."

I shivered. "Did Paul keep a diary?"

"Didn't you know?"

"No, I don't think anyone's mentioned it."

"Well, he did. For several years."

"Where is it, then?"

Father shook his head. "I'm not sure. I honestly haven't thought about it. But it must be somewhere. Probably in his—" He stopped suddenly, frowned, then smiled. "In *your* room, I mean."

"You think so?"

"Well, there, or in the attic. I really don't know."

I stared at him.

"You don't look so well," he said. "Maybe you should go back to bed. I'll be off to work again. I just wanted to see how you were."

I was embarrassed. He seldom seemed to care.

"I'll go to bed now," I murmured.

In the doorway I turned. Father smiled and nodded.

"Thanks," I said quietly.

8

The door closed. Father had left.

I was lying in my bed. My heart was pounding. I could feel my pulse thumping in my head.

Paul had kept a diary. How could I have missed that? And where could it be?

I looked around my room. The furniture was, as far as I knew, the same furniture Paul had had when the room was his. Only the bed had been changed.

Beside the bed there was a table with a drawer, and beside that an old leather armchair I seldom used. In front of the window I had a desk with a cabinet and three drawers, and to the left of the desk there were two bookshelves, one on the window wall, the other one on the wall to my parents' bedroom. Between the bookshelves and the wardrobes was my chest of drawers. That was the furniture I had in my room. The same furniture you had in your room, Paul. So, where would you have hidden your diary?

I tried to imagine myself in your place, pretended I had a diary I didn't want anyone to find. Where would I hide it?

I still had my old black sheet-metal box, my treasure box. Since I could lock it, I didn't need to hide it. Still, I used to put it aside, on the floor of one of the wardrobes, or underneath my bed.

Where have you hidden your diary, Paul?

I searched through every piece of furniture, opened every drawer, every door, felt with my fingers for a secret compartment or, maybe, a taped-up diary under something. I climbed up on my chair and checked on top of the bookshelves, but found nothing but dust. I pulled the chair to the wardrobes, only to find more dust. And I climbed up on top of the desk to reach the metal grid of the ventilator. It was absolutely stuck.

I didn't find any diary.

All I found was the plastic bag with toy cars that I had put in behind the books on the shelf a few years ago. I had actually forgotten all about it. I looked into the plastic bag and it was like traveling nine or ten years back in time.

I had saved my favorite cars. The others I had given away to my younger cousins. I turned the bag upside down and poured the cars out on my bed: a small red double-decker, a blue Hillman with a rear window you could open, a rusty Chevrolet that once was pink-colored, a dark-red horse transporter that used to belong to Paul. EXPRESS—HORSE BOX—HIRE SERVICE. Pale yellow letters. And then, the nicest of them all: a medium-blue Austin with a top steering wheel. A red plastic steering wheel. And when you turned the steering wheel, the front wheels turned. There were two plastic figures in the car, a driving teacher and his pupil. My father gave me the Austin when I was three years old, but I don't remember that. I do remember it was the finest car I had, the finest toy I ever had.

For a long while I looked at the toy cars. I touched them, and smelled them. And I did some driving with the blue Austin on top of my bedside table. The steering was still working perfectly, though the black rubber tires were a bit inelastic. They had deteriorated. Just like the rubber coating on Paul's table-tennis paddles.

I woke up when Mother got home.

"How are you?" she asked and touched my forehead.

"I'm feeling better now," I replied. "I don't think I have a temperature."

"Well, you're not hot anymore. Have you been sleeping long?"

"A couple of hours."

She looked at my bedside table where the Austin and the horse transporter were still standing.

"So, you've played with your toys, have you?" she said in a childish voice.

I smiled. "I found them on my shelf when I was looking for a book."

Mother laughed. "You don't have to explain. I understand." She took another look at the cars. "That's funny."

"What is?"

She picked up the dark-red horse transporter. "Paul got this on his third birthday. Stefan bought it for him. It came with some horses, plastic ones, which soon disappeared."

She put it back on the table. "And this one was *your* present when you had your third birthday. It was also from Stefan."

I was watching her as she spoke. I could see that obscure darkness that comes when you feel sad. Still, I thought her eyes were shining, as if she were happy anyhow.

"And here they are together on your bedside table," she continued. "The two brothers' presents for their third birthdays.

Do you remember when your car disappeared? The blue one, I mean?"

I shook my head.

"You were devastated. We thought you would never stop crying. And later, when we finally found it, you wouldn't let go of it. You took it with you everywhere. You even slept with it," she said, laughing. "Do you remember?"

"No. I just remember it was my nicest car. My favorite car."

"And now, you're playing with it again," she said teasingly, and disappeared into the kitchen.

The next evening my parents were invited to a party.

"We will probably be rather late," Mother said, "so, you will have to make do on your own."

We were sitting in the kitchen having dinner. It was the first day in a week that I did not spend in bed.

"Couldn't we ask Daniel to come over?" I asked. "If he wants to?"

Mother and Father stared at me.

"So," Mother said, "not only have you started to play with your cars, but now you want a baby-sitter. Did you really turn sixteen?"

"Just traveling in time," I said.

"There's a film on TV," said Father. "A western. You could watch it. Then you wouldn't feel bored."

"I don't care about being bored. I just want to see Daniel, that's all. And since you're going out ..."

"Of course," Mother said. "He'll be glad to come. Go ahead and call him."

"I will," I said, and saw my father's face darken.

9

I sat down next to Daniel.

"It's been a long time since I was here," he said. "I'm glad you called."

He glanced at the flickering screen.

"I believe that's the hero," he said and pointed toward the television. A middle-aged man with an extraordinarily dull face was slowly riding into town. He was chewing on a straw and talking to his horse. "Now we'll have a good rest in this peaceful place, Blackie," he said, smiling at a couple of tarts outside the local whorehouse.

"God, I'm tired of this crap." Daniel sighed. "Mendacious bloody crap, that's what it is."

"I'll turn it off, if you want. I don't care."

I put on a record, leaned back on the couch and glanced at Daniel. He was looking at everything: the paintings, the furniture, the ugly floor vase we never managed to get rid off. Then he felt my looking at him and turned.

"What are you thinking of?" he asked.

"I'm thinking of you," I answered, a bit too quickly.

He laughed. "Me? Why?"

I was already regretting what I had said. It was all thoughts, nothing I knew or needed to know.

"What were you thinking?" he repeated.

"Oh, it's nothing. Just a stupid thought."

"Stupid? About me?" His smile was a bit uncertain. "Now you will really have to explain what you mean, Jonas."

I hesitated for a long time before I dared to speak.

"Daniel, were you in love with Paul?"

I had thought there would be an obvious reaction, but it never came. He just turned away from me, slowly, focusing on the large Miró reproduction hanging over the TV.

"In love," he said quietly. "Yes, perhaps I was. Perhaps I was in love with your brother, although I'm not sure it really was ... being in love. I mean, maybe ... maybe I was just lonely, and it's so easy to imagine things if you're lonely. And Paul ..."

He turned and looked at me. "Have you heard things? About me?"

I shook my head.

"So, you were just guessing ..."

"More or less," I whispered.

He lit a cigarette, and I got up to open the balcony door. I glanced at Paul's picture as I passed the television, to see if he was happy or sad.

"He used to visit me quite often," Daniel said. "I liked seeing him, talking with him. I liked looking at him. Perhaps I would also have liked to ... Well, I'm not all that experienced when it comes to physical love. It seems so overrated ..."

"Did Paul know?" I asked. "About your being ..."

"I don't know. I guess he did. You notice things like that.

"You mustn't believe I was interested in every boy or man I met. Quite the opposite, I guess. I wasn't attracted to more than a few. What I missed was more ... How can I put it? I missed *someone.* Not just anyone. And Paul … Well, he was in a way both young and adult. Both boy and man. I was confused by him. I'd known him since he was born, but it was only during his transition period I started to— You know he liked painting, but he also liked photography. He had, on the whole, a feeling for pictures, the power to create pictures. His marks in art were always the best. And so, when I bought a camera, by the end of '68 I believe, Paul wanted us to take 'real' pictures. He wanted to take pictures other than of birthday parties and beautiful views, he said. He wanted to take artistic pictures.

"He came to me one day in January the year he died. I think it was a Sunday. We were going to take portrait pictures. I had rigged up some sheets for background, and I had borrowed some photo lights from a neighbor.

"Paul was whistling when he came in. I could hear him from the stairs. He was excited and happy and wanted us to start at once. But first he told me what kind of pictures he wanted to take."

"What did he say?"

"He wanted pictures of me. He wanted me to take off my shirt. He said clothes were disturbing. And so we started. He took a whole lot of pictures. Some you could clearly see were me. But in others, you could only see parts of a body, a neck, a shoulder. Sometimes just a few lines, a form.

"He seemed satisfied. He had taken the pictures he wanted. 'Now it's your turn, Daniel,' he said. And took off his sweater. He had such a beautiful body. I can see him now, all the lines, the soft lines.

"I started to photograph him. But I felt guilty looking through the viewfinder. As if I were using him, even though the idea was his from the start. But he didn't know what I felt. At least I hadn't told him. And I was all confused, seeing this half-naked boy in front of me. I took pictures of his face, his chest, his shoulders. I took the same kind of pictures he had taken of me. Not that I had any thoughts of creating art. No, I just wanted to see his body.

"And then ... then suddenly Paul told me he would take off all his clothes, if I wanted to take nude photos."

Daniel went silent, and I didn't want to disturb him.

"Perhaps I shouldn't tell you this," he said after a while. "It already feels like I've told you too much. But it doesn't matter anymore. I don't know for sure if I was in love with Paul in an amorous way, but I did love him, and when I think about this, I feel confused. I don't really remember what happened. I don't really remember *what* I wanted. But I surely loved your brother. That I did. And I don't feel ashamed when I tell you I was attracted by him, by his body, of course, but that was not all. His character, his *being* attracted me. There was a sensual thing about him, almost overpowering, and it was almost too much for me when he said I could take nude photos of him. He was only a boy. A child. Even though this child meant more to me than any adult ever had. He was sitting on my floor, with his chest bare, and his beautiful dark eyes looking at me, and said I could take nude photos of him, if I wanted to.

"I murmured some blurry answer. And Paul said he wanted to take nude photos of *me*." Daniel shook his head. "That was too much. So I went into my bathroom to hide. I had to get away from him for a while. I was so afraid he'd see how excited I was. Who knows what would have happened."

"Perhaps he would have liked it," I said.

"Yes, perhaps, but I was so afraid it would ruin our friendship. He was just a boy. What if we had done something that frightened him ... No, I didn't dare risk it."

"So what did you do?"

"I stayed in the bathroom for a while. Then I went out to him. He had taken off all his clothes. He was sitting naked on the couch, waiting for me. He smiled. He had a glass of lemonade in his hand. And *that* was, in a way, just another confirmation of the fact that he was just a kid. 'How would you like me to pose?' he asked. And I stuttered something, I don't remember what. And Paul got up and placed himself in front of the sheet. I hid behind the camera, looking at his body through the viewfinder. Feeling an urge to touch him ..."

Daniel looked out the opened balcony door. The record had ended and I could hear the ticking of the kitchen clock.

"Did you take any pictures?" I finally asked.

"Yes, I did. But only one."

"Have you still got it?"

He nodded.

"Can I see it?"

"Yes, of course. You can see it when you're at my place."

"Why did you take only one picture?"

There was a sound. I couldn't tell if it was a laugh or a snort.

"I was saved by the bell," said Daniel. "Or *by* Bell. You see, the telephone rang.

"Now I can see how funny it was. But then I felt nothing but relief. Someone was calling and asking me out for a movie. And thanks to that call, there were no more nude photos. Paul giggled and got dressed. He said we could continue some other day, but I knew it would never happen. I would never dare."

We didn't speak for several minutes. Then I broke the silence.

"Did you know Paul kept a diary?"

"Yes, of course."

"Have you any idea where it might be?"

Daniel laughed and caressed my cheek.

"No, Sherlock, I don't. I haven't even the slightest idea. I thought *you* were the one who found clues and solved problems in this story."

"Perhaps I *have* been too secretive," Daniel said as we stood in the hallway. "I mean, in general." He turned toward me. "You're nice. I like talking with you. I like being with you. And it keeps getting nicer. You're growing up."

"I like you too, Daniel," I said. And hugged him.

10

I was lying in bed reading when my parents came back from the party.

"The light is still on in Jonas's room," I heard my mother whisper.

"I'm awake," I shouted.

I could hear them hang up their coats. And I heard my father's footsteps as he went hastily to the bathroom. Next, my mother stood in the doorway to my room.

"Hi, love. Have you been alone for long?"

"No. Daniel left half an hour ago, or so."

"What were you doing?"

"Talking."

There was a flush from the bathroom. Then Mother went out, and Father came in and sat on the bed.

"Did you have fun?" I asked.

"I guess," he replied. "It was okay. What about you? Did you see the film?"

"No."

"Why not?"

"It was boring. Predictable, I guess."

He looked at me. "I thought it was good when I was young. I went to a matinee." He paused. "What did you do, then?"

"Listened to music. Talked."

"About what?"

"All sorts of things," I lied. "This and that. Nothing special."

My father was sad. I changed position, and as I turned, my hand just happened to land on his arm. Just like that.

At first he stiffened. Then he put a hand on my hand and gently held it.

"Are you all right now?"

"Yes, more or less."

He looked away and spotted the cars.

"So you've taken out your toys again." He reached for the blue Austin. "I bought this for your third birthday. At the toy shop down by the harbor. I bought it during my lunch break."

"Why did you choose that one?"

"Don't you like it?" he asked, surprised.

I giggled. "Of course I do. It was my finest car. I really like it."

"Yes, so do I," Father said. "That's why I bought it. It was the nicest one they had. Do you remember when you hid it and we couldn't find it? You were unhappy for days. Do you remember?"

"No, but Mum has told me about it."

"And then we found it inside the base to one of the wardrobes in the hall. Behind that base front that always fell off when your mother was vacuuming."

I was suddenly tense. "No, I don't remember. What base front?"

"The one covering the base," Father explained. "The base front. They all fell off every now and then, until I screwed them on. You don't remember? The base front must have fallen off that day too, I guess. Anyway, you used the open base as a garage for your cars. And then I guess Mum or I put the front plate back in place without checking if anything was left inside. That's why we didn't find the Austin until the next week."

I couldn't sleep. I was too excited. By my side—on my bedside table—stood the blue Austin. I thought it shimmered, like some magic item. And the medium-blue color, which I had never really liked, was suddenly beautiful.

I looked at my two wardrobes, looked down at the white base fronts. My brother, too, grew up in this apartment, in this room. He, too, played with his cars in the hallway. Perhaps he had also used the wardrobe bases in the hall as garages for his cars, for his dark-red horse transporter.

I got up and sneaked over to the wardrobes. I could hear sniffing and soft snoring from my mother and father's bedroom. I sat down and looked at the white bases. And I didn't see any screws.

Carefully I examined the base fronts. They seemed to be stuck. And I didn't dare use any tool. That would surely wake my parents.

I went back to bed.

I woke up late. Father had gone to some archery contest. Mother would be home all day, and I wanted to be alone when I opened the bases.

In the early afternoon Mother asked me how I felt. "You seem so restless," she said. "Is it something special?"

"No, not at all," I lied. "It's nothing."

She looked searchingly at me. "Perhaps you're still not well."

"I think I need some fresh air. I think I'll go out for a little walk."

Daniel smiled as he opened the door.

"So you're a field-worker today. Come in!"

"I'd like to see the photograph," I said, and sat down on the couch.

Daniel moved some large art books on the shelf and pulled out an old black-painted wooden box. Daniel's treasure box, I thought.

He brought it and sat down next to me, turning the box so I couldn't see inside when he opened it. He searched for a moment, then took out the picture and handed it to me.

"Here it is," he said softly. The delivery was almost ceremonial.

It was you, Paul.

You are standing in front of a rigged-up sheet. Soft lights and shadows play on the fabric behind you. You are stretching as if you had just waked. You are lifting your arms, holding your hands behind your neck, the elbows raised on each side of your head. It looks like wings when I half-close my eyes. Your chest and abdomen jut out a bit. Your right leg stands firm while your left foot is lifted, only the toes touching the floor. You are stretching yourself, and in this movement your body is turned just a bit. Your eyes are half-closed. You are smiling.

"Did you set up this picture?" I asked Daniel.

"No. No one set it up. I was just standing there looking at him, and Paul stretched. And I snapped. Click! That's all."

"It's really nice," I said.

"He was a nice boy," said Daniel.

"Have you got any copies?"

"Yes, I think so. Why? Do you want one?"

"Yes, I'd love to have one."

"Okay. Just don't show it to ..."

"No, of course not. I won't show it to anyone."

Daniel leaned over, looking at the picture. "Can you understand why he confused me? Can you understand I didn't know what to do? That I didn't dare get close to him?"

"Yes," I said quietly. "I understand."

"Look how beautiful he is. He ... You look more and more like him."

I could sense that I hurt him when I replied:

"I don't think we're that much alike. Just similar. I remind you of him, that's all. But I believe those who met him, those who knew him, mix up their memories of Paul with me, with my face, with my body, and my gestures. That's why you think we're alike."

"I don't mean to say you look just like him," Daniel said. "You have your own looks, your own ways. And those differ quite a lot from Paul's. But still ... You have, by the way, only seen pictures of him, so it's probably more difficult for you to see the likeness. You never saw him move, you never saw his gestures. You never heard his voice."

"I know," I said, "but I've been thinking about him a lot. And I've heard a lot about him. And in my dreams I have seen him move. But I haven't heard his voice. I've often wondered about that. Paul never talks to me in my dreams. It's more like I sense what he's trying to say. But you've heard him talk. You've heard his voice. How did it sound? What was it like?"

"Like yours," said Daniel.

"I too have some pictures to show," I said.

"Really? What pictures?"

First I handed him the two pictures of that other boy.

"Who's this?"

"I believe it's the other boy. The one from Czechoslovakia. He who had a name that started with M. I'm almost certain it's him. Look at this. On the back. I believe it's Czech."

"*Mému malému Princi* " Daniel read. "Yes, I guess it is."

"Do you recognize him?"

He shook his head. "No, I don't think I do. It is, of course, an old photo, but I can't remember ever having seen him before."

Then I gave him the picture of Paul in front of his desk.

Daniel smiled. "This boy I do recognize. But I've never seen this photo. Where did you find it?"

"In the attic."

"I see."

"Is that the diary he's holding?"

Daniel held the picture close to his eyes. "Well, I don't know. I don't remember what it looked like. He must have had several. He was writing for years."

And finally I gave him the picture of Paul on his way out of the bathroom.

Daniel smiled. "He looks just like a little boy. If it wasn't for …"

"Yes, I know."

"But where was it taken? It's not at your place."

"No. I guess it's where the other boy lived. At M's place. I believe *he* took the picture."

Mother was reading when I got home.

"You've been gone a long time."

"Yes. I stopped in to see Daniel on my way home."

She glanced at me and frowned. "Come, let me look at you. You still look a little pale."

She put her hand on my forehead. "You're still a bit hot, Jonas. I think you'd better lie down. You don't look well. You shouldn't have been out so long. I think it's best you stay home from school tomorrow. Don't you agree?"

"Yes," I said, "I do."

And I think the smile was still on my face when I fell asleep.

11

The door closed. Mother had left.

I sat down on the floor in front of the wardrobes in my room. For a long while I just sat there looking at the white painted bases. I still didn't dare examine them. What if I was wrong?

The left wardrobe was standing in the corner next to the wall to the hall. That made it difficult to get hold of the front plate. I took hold of the right base front. It was stuck, didn't move a bit. I knocked on it. Yes, it appeared to be just as hollow as the bases in the hallway.

I leaned forward and checked the side of the base. There was a very narrow opening between the front plate and the base itself. I went to get a knife.

Carefully I wedged the point of the blade into the slit. One millimeter, two, three. Then I hit the handle with my hand, and the front plate moved a little.

I forced half the blade into the widened opening, prying it back and forth, back and forth. Then I hit the handle one more time with my hand, and suddenly the front plate popped down in front of my knees.

My heart stopped.

My hand was shaking as I put away the knife. I leaned forward and looked into the open base. Dust, dust, dust. And a couple of silverfish trying to escape the daylight I had let in. And behind the dust and the silverfish was a cardboard box.

I whooped.

Then I pulled out the box.

Someone had made it lower by cutting off a few centimeters. It fit the base perfectly. Letters from some trademark that had been halved in the cutting covered the long sides of the box, but I couldn't make out the words. There were no letters on the lid, though someone had drawn a skull and crossbones on the brownish surface.

I had found Paul's treasure box.

I smiled at the box as if it were a living thing, a loved thing. Then I swept away the dust, put the front plate temporarily back in place, and got back in bed.

I shivered in anticipation as I felt the weight of the box. I took off the lid. And there it was, the diary. Together with some letters, photos, and other papers. For almost eighteen years, the box had waited for me. Dust and dirt from eighteen years had covered the narrow opening to Paul's hiding-place. But I had found it.

Carefully I took up the diary. It was the same notebook Paul held in his hand in the photo I had found in the attic. Or at least it was a similar one. A handwritten label decorated the cover, but this time it was not in my mother's hand. This must be your handwriting, Paul, I thought, and read:

Paul Lundberg. Diary No. 4. 24 December 1968.

"This must be your last diary," I whispered.

I put the notebook aside and took out the rest of the contents. There were—among other things—two pictures of the other boy. The first seemed to be a school photograph. He was looking straight into the camera, his neck slightly bent, a smile on his lips. The other picture—a full-figure color photograph—showed him on a beach. He was standing at the waterline in a yellow robe. He was laughing for the photographer, holding his arms straight out from his body. Like a cross, I thought. The robe had slid open, partly revealing his naked body.

I turned over the photo. And this time it was the same handwriting as in the letter that I had found in the attic. *Mému malému Princi. Tvůj Milenec.*

"Milenec!" I whispered. "So that's your name. What happened to you when Paul ... when Princi died?"

I took out the three letters. They were all addressed to Paul. And it was Milenec's handwriting.

I leaned back in bed. The room seemed to revolve around me, around and around. I felt all dizzy. And confused.

For the first time I had doubts about my investigation. Did I really have the right to poke about in my brother's hidden things? Did I really have the right to search out my brother's secrets? And if I did, who—or what—was it that gave me the right?

I closed my eyes, whispered your name, hoping you would speak to me in one way or another, that you would give me your approval.

But I didn't hear a thing.

Suddenly I got up and went into the kitchen. The leftovers from my breakfast were still there. I turned on the radio and cleared the table. Then I filled the sink with water and washed the dishes.

Half an hour later I returned to my room. I noticed that one of the letters had fallen from my bed when I got up.

I went over and picked it up. As I did so, two words caught my eye: "*...means brother ...* "

My heart beat faster. I began to read:

Ahoj můj Bratře!
I dream of you all day. Not to mention the nights. So I just had to write you, Princi. "Bratr" means brother in Czech. Mother has told me about a couple of guys (who were lovers) she knew back in Prague. They used to call each other "bratr". So I guess you could say that you and I for the first time got ourselves a brother. Ahoj můj bratře! (Hello my brother!) And don't forget to ask your parents about letting you stay at my place on the Walpurgis Night.
See you on Friday. Love!
P.S.

I laughed. That was the sign I had been waiting for. Paul had got himself a brother. And you can tell everything to your brother.

I turned over the letter. The backside was blank.

"Why do you write 'P.S.' when there's no postscript, Milenec?"

I lay down on the bed with the other two letters.

Ahoj Paul!
Today I told Mother about you. She seemed a bit sad at first, but when I had told her more about you and what I felt she became

happier. But she doesn't think I should tell Dad. Not yet, anyway. She said she'd help me to tell it to him later on. And then she asked how much I love you. "Stává se smrtelně důležitym," I replied. She just laughed. (It means I can't live without you, Princi.) And so she told me about those guys she knew in Prague. But it's hard to be "bratr" in Czechoslovakia. There's too much prejudice. I guess it's even harder now with the new Soviet regime.

Before I was worried about being "bratr". Sometimes I was even sad. But now, ever since I met you, I don't bother at all.

All for now. See you soon, můj bratře!

Milenec

I folded the letter and put it back. And so I took out the third, and last, letter. After a short while I realized this must have been the first letter Milenec wrote to my brother.

Hi, Paul!

I'm so happy Mister Håkansson persuaded me to model in your class. Otherwise we may never have met. And I could feel there was something special about you as soon as I entered the class-room. And I could feel you watching me. Only I hardly dared look at you. It was tough as it was sitting all naked before your class. I'd never expected I'd be so nervous. We've always been very relaxed about nakedness in my family. But it was something completely different, sitting naked on the teacher's desk in front of a class. Especially after I'd seen you entering the room. I could for some reason sense you were just like me. Did you feel that too?

And I was so glad to run into you outside the school afterwards.

I dreamed of you, both that night and yesterday night. Mum and Dad told me I seem so happy. But I didn't dare to tell them why. They don't know. I will tell them, some day.

The picture I send you with this letter was taken in school last year. I thought you would like to have it. I would be really glad if I could have one picture of you.

I want to see you again, Paul. Soon, that is. Perhaps we could meet in town on Saturday. We could go for a walk or something. Perhaps we could meet at the pedestrian street outside the department store around half past ten. Call me if you can't make it. But I hope you will.

I like you, Paul.

Love, Petr!

"Petr?" At first I was confused. "Petr? But your name is Milenec!"

I took out my treasure box and looked for the pictures of Milenec. "Damn! Daniel's got them."

Then my mind cleared and I remembered the page where one of the pictures had been.

"Yes, that's it." It was beside that picture that I had seen the name. *"Down by the bay. March 1969. Petr je tady."*

I smiled and felt really happy. The way you must have felt, Paul, when you saw the three fox cubs.

I looked at my alarm clock. Twenty minutes to two. Great! The library would soon be open.

"Have you got a Czech-Swedish dictionary?" I asked the woman at the counter.

She took off her glasses and looked at me. "No, I don't think we do, but I'll check for you."

She browsed through the card catalog. "No, I'm sorry, we don't, but we do have a Czech-English dictionary in the reference section. Will that do?"

"Yes," I said.

"But I'm afraid you can't take it out. We don't lend the reference books."

"That's all right. I just want to look up a few words."

I browsed through the book.

Látka, lhář, lump, matematika, mimořadny …

"It must be here somewhere."

I scanned the lines. And right there—in the middle of the page—I found it:

milenec / mi-le-nets / m. lover

"Lover!" I laughed. Milenec was not a name. Milenec was the nickname my brother had used for his friend.

"Lover," I whispered. "The Prince and his lover."

12

I forced myself not to open Paul's diary until Friday evening. Mother and Father were watching a film on television. For a while I sat with them in the living room.

"I don't think I'll stay," I said, and stood up. "I'm going to bed to read. Sleep well."

They looked surprised.

"It's just half past nine," said my father.

"You're not ill again, are you?" asked my mother.

"No, I'm fine. Just a little tired. Good night!"

I arranged the pillows against the headboard, undressed and nestled down in bed with your diary in my hands.

Tuesday, 24 December 1968.

It's almost one o'clock at night, and actually Wednesday. We've been at Grandma's and Grandpa's earlier today. I gave them a candlestick I made in school. Grandma gave me a sweater and Grandpa gave me a book. We had coffee, then we went home. Daniel came in the afternoon. We had Christmas dinner, and after that Daddy said he wanted to take a walk. But I told him I don't need Santa anymore. I'm fifteen. Mum and Daniel just laughed, but Dad looked a bit sad. At least he delivered all the gifts. He gave me this diary and the musical "Hair" on LP. Mum had bought me a pair of jeans, but I will have to change them. Too big. Daniel is trying to make me like jazz. He gave me a Dave Brubeck album. It's quite good, actually. But it's a bit strange, this Christmas thing. I liked it when I was small. Now it's more of an effort.

Friday, 27 December 1968.

Went to town with Dad in the morning. I changed the jeans for a neater pair. We had coffee at Nilsson's cafe before we separated. I met Elisabeth and Carina on the square. They want me to come with them to a party at Anders's place on New Year's Eve. But I told them I'm busy. I don't want to see either Göran or Janne after what happened at the Lucia party. Tonight I went to see Daniel for a while. He showed me his new camera. Nikon. We talked about taking pictures of each other soon. I wanted to speak to him about THAT, but there was no time. It's not only that he's not dating any girls. It's something else too. More like a feeling. And although he's that much older than I am, he feels like a mate. Almost like a big brother.

Paul sometimes wrote about things my mother and father had told me about. Nothing special, just things. He mentioned Daniel quite often.

Daniel was wrong about the day when they took the pictures. It was not on a Sunday. It was Friday, 17 January 1969. And Paul's story differed slightly from what Daniel had told me:

… Then Daniel said I was beautiful. That he likes my eyes. I didn't know what to say. He said he wanted to take pictures of me, but not just of my face. I asked what he meant, and finally he told me he wanted to take nude pictures of me. I was astonished at first, but then I thought it would be fun. But I was really nervous. Undressed while he visited the bathroom. But he only took one picture before the phone rang …

I continued my reading. And smiled as I read about an event at the end of February 1969. Paul had written about how our father had wanted to screw the front plates onto the wardrobe bases, *"but I said I wanted to be alone in my room, and that he would have to do it another day. Or I can do it myself. He seemed a bit irritated but agreed. Hopefully he will forget all about it. If not, I will have to find a new hiding-place. Or I will have to do with the other one."*

So he did have another hiding-place. I had thought so, since I had found only his fourth diary. The other books couldn't have just disappeared. But I was certain the other hiding-place was not in my room.

Then I found the first note on Petr. Or Milenec.

Thursday, 13 March 1969.

What an incredible day! The last period was a double lesson in Art. Håkansson told us we'd do something we'd never done before. We'd draw from a model. And I thought we were to draw each other. But as we entered the other room there was a guy waiting for us. He looked so fine I just blushed. He was wearing a thick dressing gown, and when Håkansson was through talking, he took off the gown and sat on the desk. And he was completely nude. I just stared. He seemed in a way even more naked than the guys do in the locker room. I had a hard-on. And I was shaking when I started to draw. But Håkansson was satisfied with my drawing, although he thinks I draw too beautifully. Again I blushed. Sometimes I think he understands. And then, after school, I met the boy who was modeling. He came out from the candy shop just as I was about to go in. "Hello," he said and smiled. I just nodded. And blushed …

I don't think I ever read a text that fast. And I've never read anything as exciting as the diary from the last six months of my brother's life. After my mother came in to say good night, I continued to read. When I had read the entire diary I was absolutely shaken.

I browsed back, reread some of it. The pulse was throbbing in my head and I believe I cried.

I had to go to the bathroom. My face was absolutely pale in the mirror. My eyes were red. I dabbed my face with cold water to revive.

The clock in the kitchen was half past two. It had started to get light outside the window.

I turned off the bedside lamp, pulled the blanket over me, and closed my eyes. But I'm not sure whether I was awake or asleep. My eyes were closed, but inside my head the story was once more being told, the story of my brother Princi and his lover.

13

"**Where are** you going, Paul?" one of his classmates shouted.

"I'm going down to the candy store. Then I'm taking the bus to town. I'm gonna do some shopping. See you tomorrow."

He cut through the schoolyard and took the footpath down to the road and the candy store.

Just as he was reaching for the doorknob, the door opened.

"Hi!"

Paul looked up. "Hi!" he stuttered and blushed.

"I saw you earlier in the classroom," said the other boy. "What's your name?"

"Paul."

"I'm Petr."

"Petr?"

The other one laughed. "Yes, Petr. But most of the people here call me Peter. They probably think Petr sounds a bit strange and cut off. It's a Czech name. Or rather, the Czech form of Peter. That's where I come from."

"Have you been here long?" Paul asked.

"Nine years."

They became silent, and Paul looked down at the ground.

"I thought you were going to shop."

"What? Yes, of course. Wait a second," said Paul and went into the store.

When he came out he felt more relaxed. And Petr was standing waiting for him.

"Are you going home?" he asked, offering Petr a toffee.

"I don't know. I think so. Where are you going?"

"To town. Not for any special reason. Just to look around."

"Can I come along?"

"We could have a coffee at the cafe by the harbor," Petr said as they got off the bus. "If you feel like it."

"Sure."

Paul was still rather confused. He couldn't really understand that he had made contact with the other boy. They walked side by side, Paul trying to keep in step with Petr. Now and then he glanced at him. What incredible eyes, he thought.

Petr felt Paul looking at him and turned toward him and smiled.

They were sitting at one of the window tables with a view of the harbor. Petr was pointing to one of the large cranes.

"That's where my father works," he said. "In that green crane."

"Have you ever been up there?"

"No, it's terribly high. I wouldn't dare," Petr said with a laugh. "Would you dare to climb up?"

"Yes, I think I would. It would be fun."

Then they went silent.

"How was your drawing of me?" Petr asked, after a while.

Paul smiled, a bit embarrassed, and looked out the window. "Well, I don't know. Mr. Håkansson says he thinks it's too beautiful."

Petr was laughing. "Too beautiful? What did he mean?"

"Well, he didn't say that exactly, but something like that. I'm not really sure what he meant."

"Do you think it's too beautiful?"

Paul hesitated. "No. It doesn't look like you at all."

Petr laughed again and reached for Paul, who blushed at the touch, worried that someone might have seen.

"What are you afraid of?"

Paul shrugged.

"There's nothing to be afraid of," the other boy continued. "The worse thing that can happen would be if people who really have nothing to do with us would begin to talk rubbish. But since they don't have anything to do with us, we don't really have to care, do we?"

Paul was still silent.

Petr then leaned on the table and whispered: "Hey, I saw you as soon as you entered the drawing-class room. And it felt like … as if we were alike. As if we *are* alike. And I knew I wanted to get to know you. I think we can be pals. Friends. See?"

Paul nodded, and thought his heartbeats must be heard even by the woman at the counter in the other room.

"I'd love to make friends with you," Petr continued, "if you want to."

"I do."

They were walking by the harbor. Petr was talking about his parents. He said they would like to go back to Czechoslovakia, but that it was impossible after the Soviet invasion.

"Did you flee from Czechoslovakia?"

"No. We moved out. To Germany, first. Where Dad got a job in Hamburg, at the harbor. That's where he learned to handle cranes. A year later we moved here. We had planned to stay just a year or so, but it got longer. And then, last year, Czechoslovakia was invaded by the Soviets, and now we must stay."

"Why can't you return?"

"Well, we can, if we want. But there's so much trouble there. You never know what will happen. It's too unstable. Soldiers and policemen everywhere. I don't want to go back there. Not yet, at least. And my mum and dad also want to stay here. So far."

They sat down on a bench by the small fish market.

"I had an accident with my bicycle here once," said Paul and pointed to the railroad track. "I turned around to look at a ... to look at someone I recognized, and I didn't see the track. And the front wheel got stuck and I fell. An old lady came to help me. And I cried. Not that it hurt that much, but because I had ruined my new jacket."

Petr was watching Paul's face as he talked, and didn't seem to be listening.

"Now I know!" he suddenly burst out.

"What?" Paul wondered.

"I had a feeling you reminded me of someone, even when I first saw you. I couldn't figure out who it was, but now I remember."

"Who is it?"

"You remind me of a boy in a book my grandmother used to read to me when we were still living in Prague. A fairy tale, it was. With beautiful pictures."

"What was it about?"

"*O malém princi.*"

"What did you say?"

"It was a tale about a young prince," Petr said and smiled.

A couple of days later Paul was sitting on the parking lot fence on the square, waiting for Petr. He had received a letter in which Petr wrote he would like to see him. Paul's mother had giggled when she saw him reading it. "Have you got a girlfriend?" she had asked. "You seem so happy." But he had just laughed.

He looked at his watch. Eleven o'clock, Petr had said, and now it was ten past. What if he didn't come?

He looked toward the bus stop every time he heard a bus. But he didn't yet know where Petr lived, and therefore he didn't know which bus he would arrive on.

Suddenly there was a warm breath on his neck. And before he had time to turn around he heard a voice saying, "I think I'm falling in love with you."

Paul felt a glow spread in his body. "What did you say?" he asked as Petr jumped over the fence.

"You heard me," Petr said. "I thought it was best I told you at once. Before you even saw me. Otherwise I may not have dared."

Paul laughed and got down from the fence. "Yes, I did hear."

"Well?" said Petr. "Aren't you supposed to say something?"

"Me? Why?"

Petr waved his arms. "They always do in the movies."

Paul smiled and pulled out a piece of paper from one of his jacket pockets. "Let's pretend it's a silent movie," he said and mimed "Here you go!"

Petr unfolded the paper.

I am the other one
the one who has been waiting so long
for something I never thought would happen
I am the other one;
he who has been waiting for you
I think we are
     friends

Petr looked up at Paul, then he leaned close and gave him a quick kiss on the cheek.

"Don't be afraid, Paul," he whispered. "Look around you. People are all too busy. Nobody cares about us. And even if they see us, it doesn't matter. You are the one who's been waiting. You and me. And if we have waited this long, there's no reason why we should stop ourselves from doing what we want. See?"

"Yes, of course," Paul replied, "but I still feel a bit uneasy. Not because of you, maybe, but because of everybody else. I would … I want to be alone with you. Just you and me, I mean. For ourselves."

Petr nodded. "So do I," he said. "We can go to my house. Mum and Dad are visiting a friend this afternoon. They won't be home till late tonight. We'll be on our own."

Petr opened the front door and rushed inside.

"I have to go to the loo. It's urgent!"

Paul went into the kitchen and sat down at the table. He heard the flush from the toilet, followed by a door being opened.

"Where are you?" Petr yelled.

"In the kitchen. There's a note for you on the table."

"What does it say?" Petr asked, coming in.

"It says, '*Petr. Jdeš … jdeš mi na ner … nervy.*' No, I can't read it."

Petr laughed and took the note.

"What does it say?" Paul wondered.

"It's Mum. She's a bit sour because I forgot to clean up after my breakfast. I don't usually forget, but I was excited about seeing you."

"Is she mad?"

"No, not at all. Just a little. She thinks I'm getting on her nerves. That's all." He sat down opposite Paul. "Do you want anything? Coffee? Tea?"

Paul shook his head.

"Nothing at all?"

"No, nothing."

"Are you sure?"

Paul laughed. "Yes, I'm sure. Why are you nagging me? Are you going to ruin my nerves too?"

"No, I just thought perhaps you wanted something."

"Like what?"

"Like me," said Petr. And smiled. "Come, I'll show you the house."

Paul's attention was caught by a picture hanging on the living-room wall. It was a portrait of a young man with dark eyes. His smile reminded him of Petr's.

"Is that a relative?"

"No," Petr said. "It's Jan Palach. The boy who burned himself to death a couple of months ago."

"What? What do you mean?"

"He burned himself to death in the middle of January. As a protest against the new regime in Czechoslovakia."

Paul stared at the picture. "Where did it happen?"

"In Prague. At the *Václavské náměsti*. That's a large square. It was just outside the National Museum, beside the statue. But he didn't die at once. People put out the fire, and he was brought to the hospital. A couple of days later he died."

"Jesus! That's totally insane! He can't be much older than us. Or is it an old picture?"

"No, I don't think it's old," answered Petr. "He was not that old. Twenty, I think. Just a few years older than me. My mother framed the picture. She got it from a magazine. He's almost like a saint back in Czechoslovakia. People are making pilgrimages to the Vaclav place and to Jan Palach's grave, to honor his memory and to demonstrate against the regime." He was silent for a moment. "We had a letter from Grandma the week after he died. She and Grandpa were nearby when it happened. They reached the statue by the time the ambulance arrived, and the smell of petrol and burnt flesh was awful."

"Did your grandmother know him?"

Petr shook his head. "I don't think so. Perhaps she knew who he was, but I don't know. He was not from Prague, but from some small village. My cousin Sasa, who was in the same students' union as Palach, knew him. He took part in the hunger strike outside the National Museum after Palach's death. My uncle forced him to stop. They were afraid they would lose Sasa too."

"Did it lead to anything good? After he had burned himself to death, I mean."

"No, I don't think so. Well, yes, maybe. Perhaps it made people get together, made them understand the seriousness of the situation. But those who really should have listened to the demonstrators, the occupying power, didn't seem to care at all. They even had the nerve to say that Jan Palach was 'a victim of the bad Czech school system,' a system that obviously hadn't taught him the 'truth' about Marxism-Leninism. But according to my dad the Czech people have more than learned what that 'truth' means."

Paul was mumbling.

"What did you say?"

"I said, it's terrible that someone should believe that the only chance of making a change would be by burning himself to death. It's just like the monks in Saigon a couple of years ago. Do you remember? They also burned themselves to death. People were even filming them. That's insane! They must already have known that someone would burn himself to death, but instead of trying to stop the whole thing, or at least trying to put out the fire, they rigged up their cameras and started to film!"

"Yes, I know. But no one was filming Jan Palach. Nobody knew about it, except the other students. Those who also would burn themselves."

"What?"

"Yes. There were others who were supposed to burn themselves. After Palach. But it never happened. I don't know why. Perhaps they didn't dare. Or perhaps they thought Jan Palach's death had brought enough attention to the matter. I don't know. I think it was twelve or fourteen others who should've burned themselves. One after the other. They drew lots on who should start. And it was Palach. Oh, I don't want to talk about this anymore. It only makes me sad. Come, I'll show you my room."

Paul was sitting beside Petr on the bed. He looked around the unfamiliar room, his eyes constantly returning to the strange pictures on the wall over the bed. There were three of them, filled with pinned butterflies under the glass. Hundreds of butterflies.

"Do you like them?" Petr asked.

Paul hesitated before answering. "I'm not sure."

"You're not sure?"

"No. I mean, the butterflies are nice. They are really beautiful. But it's a bit horrible as well."

"Yes, I know what you mean. I can't quite make up my mind whether I like them or not," said Petr. "They were given to me by my uncle Luba. He's been collecting butterflies all his life. And so, when we moved from Prague he gave me the pictures as a farewell gift." Petr got up on his knees and pointed to one of the butterflies. "This one's the most beautiful, I think. It's from South America. They call it Silver Flash. But here it says *Argyrophorus argenteus*. It almost looks like a cabbage butterfly in this light. But now and then these wings glitter with a pearly luster. And when they fly around up in the Andes where the sunshine finds them, they flash silver. Look! It almost looks as if the wings are made of silver. It's so beautiful, don't you think?"

Then he sat down and took hold of Paul's hand. "But you're even more beautiful," he said. "You must be the most beautiful." And he leaned close and kissed him on the cheek.

Paul could feel the warmth spread in his body. He leaned back, pulling Petr with him. "Come!" he said. "Come closer."

Petr lay by his side, gently stroking Paul's eyebrow with his forefinger. "*Můj malý princi*," he whispered. "*Můj malý, malý princi.*"

Paul could feel his breath against his face. It was so warm, almost hot, as if he had a fever.

Petr smiled when he asked him. "No, I don't think I do. But if so, you're the one who's caused it."

And they kissed.

In the evening they were standing by the bus stop waiting for the bus that would take Paul home.

"We must see each other soon," said Petr, "or I'll go mad."

Paul laughed. "Of course we will see each other soon," he replied, "or I'll die."

Petr took him in his arms, and this time Paul no longer cared that someone might see them. He could feel the other boy's body close to his, and he could feel his own body reacting.

Petr could feel it too. He squeezed Paul even harder, then let go and stepped back. "This is really highly dangerous," he said, laughing.

"Yes, and oh so exciting."

14

"**There is** a letter for you," Paul's mother told him when he came home from school. "And there was a boy who wanted you on the phone. I think he said he was Peter."

"It must have been Petr," Paul said and took off his suede jacket. "Wasn't it?"

"Petr?"

"It's a Czech name."

"Yes, he might have said Petr. I'm not sure. Anyway, here's the letter."

"Thanks. Will he call again?"

"I think he said he would. Yes, I'm sure. Do I know him?"

"No, I met him recently."

"In school?"

"Yes, in school."

The telephone rang. He could hear his mother answering.

"It's for you, Paul. It's Peter ... I mean, Petr."

He seized the receiver.

"Hi, Princi! It's me."

"Hi! Thanks for the letter. But I still haven't had time to ask them about staying at your place on Walpurgis Night."

"It doesn't matter. You can ask them later. Now you will have to ask them something else. Something even more important."

"What?"

"If you can stay at my place tomorrow night."

"Tomorrow?"

"Yes. Mum and Dad will go to some friends in Kalmar. They're planning to see the hockey match between the U.S.S.R. and Czechoslovakia, and they won't be home until Saturday evening."

"Wait," said Paul. "I'll ask Mum."

A short while later he returned to the phone. "Yes, I can. When should I come?"

They were sitting in front of an open fire talking. The television was on, the match had started. But they had turned off the sound and were listening to a record.

"Mother's convinced I've gone mad," said Paul.

"Why?"

"I told her I was gonna see the match, but she knows I'm totally uninterested in hockey."

Petr laughed. "Well, you didn't lie to her. The television *is* on."

Paul leaned toward Petr and put his arm around him. "Jesus, I'm so glad I've met you."

"Yes, so am I."

"But how come you were modeling in the first place? And in our school. How did you dare?"

"Oh, it wasn't that bad," Petr said. "Mr. Håkansson asked if there was anyone in our class who would consider doing some modeling, and I raised my hand. Of course I didn't realize I'd be so nervous. Still, it wasn't that bad." He smiled and touched Paul's lips. "And I had a feeling I was going to see you."

"You had?"

"I think I had."

"What do you mean?"

"Well, perhaps I had seen you in the school yard one day when I was meeting a friend. Perhaps I even happened to ask somebody what your name was, what class you were in, and perhaps I even happened to ask Håkansson which class he wanted me to model in."

"What do you mean? Does Mr. Håkansson work at your school as well?"

"Yes, sir. Beginning to understand, are you?"

"Yes, I guess. But I can't figure out why I didn't see you when you were visiting our school yard. I ought to have seen you."

Petr laughed. "I had only seen you once before I saw you in the drawing class. You were standing alone outside the school refectory looking at something lying on the ground. Something small. And then you kneeled and picked up whatever it was you were looking at—I couldn't see what it was—and you seemed to be completely absorbed in what you had found."

"I don't know what you're talking about," Paul said, wondering. "When was that?"

"Last autumn."

"Last autumn?"

"Yes, last autumn. Near the end of September, to be more precise."

"How can you be so sure?"

"Because it was the day before my birthday."

"Meaning?"

"It was the twentieth of September, 1968. I believe it was ten past noon."

Paul laughed and pushed him. "You're kidding."

"No, I promise you. It's all true."

"I'll check that later. In my diary."

Petr went to the window and pulled down the shade. He turned and smiled. "Let's put the mattress on the floor," he said. "Then we'll have more room."

And so he started to undress: sweater, jeans, socks, underpants. All naked, he walked up to Paul, put his hands on his shoulders and pulled him close.

Paul hardly dared to touch him.

"Easy," Petr whispered. "I'm not dangerous."

Paul could feel the other one's body against his. He could feel the other one's penis against his leg.

"Shouldn't you take off your clothes?" Petr asked.

"I will," he replied. "I have to pee."

Paul closed the bathroom door behind him. His heart was beating so, he thought Petr would hear it. He went to the washbasin and dabbed his face with cold water.

"Easy now," he said to himself in the mirror. "Take it easy and go in to him. It's just what you want."

Paul took off his shirt and jeans. Then he sat down on the mattress and took off his underpants and socks. Just as rapidly he disappeared under the blanket.

Petr joined him. He was smiling and moving closer.

Once again Paul could feel Petr's warm breath on his face,

and his penis against his hip. He turned on his side. Paul thought the other boy's eyes had absorbed all the soft light in the room, they were glowing so. Like drops of water in moon-light, he thought.

Their hands met, fingers playing with each other. Whose hand are you? And their penises met, like two crossed swords.

"*Můj princi,*" Petr whispered. "*Můj malý princi.*"

"What does that mean?" Paul asked, though he already knew.

Petr whispered an answer, his hands exploring Paul's body, stroking his chest, finding his navel. They were tickling, hot, examining. Their lips were so close to each other. Paul kissed him. And Petr's eyes shone when his hand found Paul's penis. He gently fondled it.

Paul caressed the other boy's shoulders and back. Their arms collided and they giggled. Paul's hand reached the other one's buttocks just as he felt Petr's hand around his penis. Petr was gently stroking him, and Paul couldn't hold himself any longer.

"Oups!" Petr whispered, smiling.

Paul gave a loud sound, his breathing jerky.

"Now you're all sticky," he whispered, touching Petr's stom-ach.

"It doesn't matter. We do have a bathroom—and a washing machine." He reached for the T-shirt hanging over the head-board, the blanket falling off him as he moved.

Paul could see Petr's body in the soft light. He touched Petr's penis, moving his hand gently down to its base. Petr sighed, let go of the T-shirt, and lay back. Paul continued to move his hand. He could hear Petr saying something, but he couldn't hear what. He rose on his elbow to see better, to move easier.

When he heard a change in Petr's breathing, he stopped and looked down at his body. "You're so fine," he whispered, then he continued.

Petr slowly turned to him, caressing him. "Oh, Paul!"

Paul touched the other boy's neck with his lips. He could feel him swallow. He kissed him, and felt something damp hitting his own neck. He had tears in his eyes when he heard Petr's breathing. It sounded like sobbing.

"Jesus!" Petr whispered. "Hold me tight! Come!"

They hugged each other hard and for a long time.

Paul giggled. "I've never felt anything like this before."

"Nor have I," said Petr. "I don't think there is anything else like this, and if there is, I don't care. This is good enough for me."

They both suddenly began to laugh.

Petr stretched, and moved closer to Paul. "This is absolutely wonderful. What if they all knew?"

"Who?"

"Everyone! I don't care. Just so long as they knew."

"I guess some people do know," Paul said. "Don't you think?"

"Yes, I guess. Some of them."

Paul was yawning and stretching. The clock on Petr's desk showed half past two.

"Would you like to sleep now, Princi?"

Paul nodded, humming.

"Then I'll sing you a lullaby. A lullaby my grandmother used to sing to me when I was small. Come lie down on my pillow."

Paul put his head to rest and closed his eyes. He felt as though the mattress was spinning round and round, like a merry-go-round.

And Petr started to sing in a whispering, unfamiliar way.

"Hajej můj princi a spi
jsou s tebou anděle tví ..."

But Paul was already asleep.

Paul woke up because he needed to go to the bathroom. And even before he opened his eyes he knew he was at Petr's place. He recognized the light scent of him. He could hear his breathing.

Petr's arm was resting on his chest, and he didn't want to move, but after a while he just had to. Carefully he slid out from under Petr's arm and went downstairs to the bathroom.

When he returned, he whispered, "Are you awake?"

There was no reply.

"Are you awake, Milenec?"

Petr smiled and opened his eyes. He stretched out an arm and put his hand on Paul's chest. He could feel Paul's heartbeat under his palm.

"Yes, Princi," Petr whispered. "I'm awake. And all naked. Just feel!"

Paul laughed. "Yes, I can feel it. And I'm also awake. Just feel!"

Petr carefully moved his fingers over Paul's face.

"When will your parents be back?"

"Don't worry about that."

"No, but I want to know. When will they be back?"

"Why do you ask?"

"Well, I could see you have an enormous bathtub, and I thought we might have time for a bathe before they come."

Petr giggled. "We will have time enough both for bathing and ..."

"And what?"

"Well ..."

"And what else?" Paul repeated.

"Washing the sheets."

After the bath they went for a long walk. Snow was falling. Their feet made squeaking noises.

"Why did you ask if I had ever been with somebody else before?" Petr asked.

"Well, it's so strange, everything. You do so many things. You dare to do them. You do things I haven't even dreamed of. I didn't even know you could do all those things. It's as if you're a teacher or something. And then I thought maybe someone had taught *you*. You're not even a year older than I am. Where did you learn all those things?"

Petr was silent for a moment, then said: "I don't know if I've learned that much. But I like to play. I like to think of things to do. Besides, I'm not at all sure that I am the teacher. Are you sure it's not *you*, Paul?"

Paul stopped and looked at him. "Me? But I don't know anything. I would never have thought of that ... that thing you did in the bathtub. I hadn't even kissed anyone until I met you."

"Still," said Petr, "sometimes things just happen, they just come to you. You don't always need a teacher to learn something new. Some things just come. And I don't believe— Wait! Hold still!" He took off his glove and touched Paul's cheek. "Look! An eyelash!"

He opened the upper buttons of his jacket and put his hand underneath his sweater.

"What are you doing?"

"Making a wish."

"What do you mean?"

"Well, if you find an eyelash from someone else's eyes, you should put it inside your innermost clothes. Then you make a wish."

Paul laughed. "I've never heard of that. Did you make it up?"

Petr shook his head. "No, I didn't make it up. Some things you do have to learn from someone else. And this I learned from my grandmother in Prague."

"So you mean it's some sort of Czech superstition?"

"Yes."

"So, what did you wish?"

"But you must know that you're not allowed to reveal your wishes. If you do, they will never come true, whether you're here or in Czechoslovakia. Come now. Let's get on. It's getting cold."

"Shouldn't you button your jacket, then?"

"No, it's not *that* cold."

They reached the sea. The wind was chilly, and Paul was freezing.

Petr pointed to a pavilion out on a spit. "I was sitting there two years ago, watching the house on the other side of the bay burn down. Look, over there! You can still see what's left of the chimney. Can you see it?"

Paul nodded.

"The flames were huge, and the fire spread to some trees behind the house. I was afraid there'd be a forest fire that would spread to our house."

"Weren't the firemen there?"

"Yes, they were, but I was still afraid."

"Were you alone?"

"Yes."

"How come you were inside the pavilion?"

Petr hesitated. "Well ... that pavilion was ... I guess you could call it my secret hideaway," he said. "I was there nearly every day."

"You couldn't have been much of a hider. I mean, those people who lived in the house on the other side of the bay must have seen you, mustn't they?"

"No. That house had been empty for years before it burned down. There was ... there was no one who saw me." He was pensive as he looked toward the pavilion.

"What is it? Why are you hesitating?"

"Hesitating? I'm not hesitating. I was just thinking of something ... Anyway, let's go out on the spit."

Paul squatted down next to a low rock.

Petr held the camera to his eye. Through the viewfinder he could see a boy who reminded him of the prince in the fairy tale his grandmother used to read to him when he was small. But the boy in the viewfinder was not a fairy prince. He was highly real.

And his dark hair was streaming in the hard wind, his dark eyes were looking into the camera. And he was smiling.

"I could never paint your picture," Petr said. "That's why I have to take a photo. So I can look at you even when you're not around."

Paul laughed. "I would also like to have a photo. Of you. Although I've already drawn your picture, and although I've already got that school photograph. Come, sit here on the rock."

Petr handed Paul the camera.

"It has to be a profile," Paul said. "I have to get your nose."

Petr laughed. "My nose? What do you mean? Is it that special?"

"It is."

"In what way?"

"It's the only nose I've ever seen halfway into my navel."

Petr was laughing so hard he almost fell off the rock. "Well, in that case you must see that my lips are in the picture too."

"Don't worry, your lips will be there."

15

The sun was broiling on the beach where they had arranged to meet. Paul would have preferred to take the bicycle to the rocky shore on the other side of town, but he left the decision to Petr.

"My mother's not well," Petr had told him on the phone. "She's got migraine. So I don't want to be that far away from home. I thought I could bike home around noon to see how she is. Is that all right with you?"

"Yes, of course. As long as we meet," Paul replied.

They had swum out to a raft where they were sunbathing.

"To think they will land on the moon tomorrow," said Paul. "It's really fantastic! I wish I was there too. That would really be something."

"I'm sure it would, but I don't think I would dare," said Petr.

"No? Why not?"

"Well, I don't know … It's … it's so far away. What if they can't make it back? What if something goes wrong with the rocket and they can't lift off the moon? I would never have dared risk that."

"I would," said Paul and got up on his elbows. "It wouldn't really matter. I mean, if I couldn't get back. Just think what it would be like to walk on the moon, to see the earth from above. That would make it worth the trip. It must be incredibly magnificent, and the return trip not really that important, don't you think? Couldn't you die for an experience like that?"

Petr frowned. "Absolutely not. There are lots of places and countries on earth that I would like to see. Imagine going to Africa to see all the wild animals live. Or the pyramids. Or to travel on that subterranean river floating through the Postojna cave. To just sit in the boat and look at all those stalactites."

Paul laughed. "That would be great too, but you could do that first, couldn't you? And save the trip to the moon till later, when you had seen what you wanted to see on earth. Would you go then?"

"Maybe, but I don't think so. I'd still be frightened."

"I see," said Paul, "but you do know that there are really giant disgusting spiders in caves, don't you?" He put out his hand, pretending his fingers were spider legs running over Petr's back.

Petr laughed and turned away.

Then they were back on the beach.

Paul stretched out on his towel, and Petr was standing up to change clothes.

Petr smiled. "You're really looking, aren't you?"

"Yes. You're so fine. I get this strange feeling in my stomach just by looking at you. We should really have been at your place, shouldn't we? On our own."

"We'll be on our own next weekend. Mum and Dad will drive down to Kalmar again. Then we'll have three days. And I can dress and undress all the time, if you want me to. But then, you'd better get something for that stomach of yours, or you won't survive the weekend."

"I'll let them amputate my stomach as long as I can be with you."

"Okay," said Petr, "as long as they don't cut off anything else."

He put on his clothes and bent down over Paul. "I'll be back in half an hour. Just want to make sure Mum's all right." He leaned close and kissed Paul on the cheek. "I'll bring you some ice cream on my way back. See you, Princi!"

"Good. Please hurry!"

The sun blazed down on Paul's back. He was lying with the towel covering his head, listening to all the sounds around him: children laughing, parents calling, radios blaring out tunes that seemed to blow away and come back. In the distance he could hear sirens and a bus starting up, and right by his side sat a little girl talking to her plastic duck.

He pulled off the towel, sat up on his elbows, and looked at Petr's wristwatch.

"Why doesn't he come?" he whispered. "He's been gone for over an hour."

He stood up and looked toward the road. "Hurry up, Milenec." He turned and gazed out over the water. And then he made up his mind.

Quickly he packed his and Petr's things and walked up to the bicycle. It was almost one kilometer from the beach to Petr's home if he used the road. But Paul decided to take the other way, an old forest road, more or less overgrown.

He was going as fast as he could, keeping his eyes on the road to avoid the worst bumps and hollows. He had a feeling he had forgotten something, something important, but he couldn't figure out what it was.

It was only when he got near the house that he understood what he had forgotten: the sirens. The moment he caught sight of the house and the fire trucks he realized he had been smelling the smoke for quite a while.

"Petr!" he cried, and fell over. The bicycle bar hit him in the stomach, but he didn't feel it. Quickly he got up and ran toward the house. He didn't even notice that he had to jump over Petr's tossed bike.

The flames rose high above the roof. Everywhere there were firemen with hoses pointed at the conflagration. There was a roaring sound, but he didn't know whether it came from the flames or from the fire engines.

"Petr!" he screamed again.

"For God's sake, get away from here!" a fireman yelled and seized him by the arm, pulling him aside. "What are you doing? You wanna kill yourself? Keep away from here!"

Paul fell. He tried to get up, but his legs wouldn't carry him. Once again he fell, and scraped his elbow.

Suddenly there was an enormous roar. He stared—paralyzed—at the house. He saw the firemen running away from it just as the roof collapsed. An enormous shower of sparks rained down on the garden. Paul could see a birch tree on the other side catch fire.

And then he saw the ambulance.

He got up and started to stumble toward it. His legs were heavy. Every step he took set his head throbbing. What are they doing? he thought, confused, when he saw some paramedics with a stretcher.

Someone was lying on the stretcher. One of the men in white was covering the body. Paul stopped abruptly and fell down on his knees just a few meters away. He was staring at some dark thing sticking out from under the cloth. He couldn't understand what it was. His pulse was pounding, and he had problems focusing. Then he realized with horror that the black deformed thing he saw was an arm, a terribly burned arm.

Something else caught his eye.

At first he refused to believe what he was seeing. Still, he couldn't stop staring at the feet sticking out on the stretcher.

In an echoing way—as from a dream—he heard one orderly speaking to another. And when the horrible reality slowly pushed away his unwillingness to understand, he heard:

"Dead?"

"Yes. Terribly burned."

"Hell!"

"And the other one?"

"Taken to hospital."

They lifted the stretcher and pushed it into the ambulance. Paul could see how Petr's red gym shoes moved as the stretcher was locked in place. As if the feet belonged to someone still alive.

The door closed.

Paul turned away and threw up.

He was standing in the bathroom. He couldn't remember how he'd got home, but he must have biked. He had all of the things with him. He was holding the towels and the trunks in his hands. They were still wet. Then he hung them over the bathtub to dry. As if nothing had happened.

When he turned and saw his reflection in the mirror, it all caught up with him. He fell to the floor, crying.

Later, he was standing in the hallway holding Petr's things. The wristwatch glass had broken when he fell on his bike. He smelled the towel and the swim trunks, but all he could make out was salt water and sand. Petr was gone.

He went out to the stairwell, opened the refuse chute, and threw away Petr's things.

Some hours later Paul was waked by the sound of a key in the outer door. He opened his eyes and the memory of what had happened flooded over him.

"Paul?"

His mother entered his room.

"Paul?"

He looked at her.

"Hi, love. Are you sleeping at this time of day?"

He nodded.

"What is it? Are you not feeling well?" She sat down on the edge of the bed, put her hand on his forehead. "You're absolutely hot!"

"I think I have a fever," he murmured. "I've been sleeping for a while."

"Have you taken your temperature?"

He shook his head.

"Would you like me to?"

"No. I'm feeling better already. I'll be fine."

"I hope you're not having the flu again," she said anxiously. "Now when it's finally summer, and you're enjoying your last summer vacation before going to the gymnasium. I really hope you won't be sick. Perhaps you won't be free next summer. Who knows? You may have to work during your vacation."

Paul was silent. He had closed his eyes and was enjoying the touch of her hand on his face, almost as if he were a little boy again. Or …

He tried not to think of Petr, and opened his eyes.

"What's that on your arm?" his mother cried. "There's blood everywhere!"

He touched the crusted surface with his fingers. "I fell," he managed. "It doesn't hurt anymore."

"We have to clean it," she said. "By the way, did you go swimming?"

He closed his eyes and slowly nodded.

"Perhaps you would like to sleep some more?"

"Yes, I think I would. For a while, at least."

"I'll wake you before dinner. Is that okay?"

"Fine."

She stood up, ready to leave.

"No, wait!" Paul cried.

"Honey, what's the matter?"

He seized her hand. "Can't you wait till I'm asleep?"

"Yes. Yes, of course I can," she replied. "Of course I'll stay."

16

The last notes in my brother's fourth diary were written late at night before Monday, 21 July 1969. Briefly he describes the terrible things that had happened. But then, at the end, there is a change in his writing. The sentences get longer.

I'm at home. In bed. Or sitting on top of my desk looking out the window. Without really seeing. At least I don't know what I see. I can't understand he's dead. Try to think of something else but always return to Petr. Or to emptiness. Mum thinks I'm sick, and I let her. I can't tell her of Petr's death. At least not yet. There's too much to explain. I'm afraid she wouldn't understand. Or Dad. But I want them to know about Petr and me. Jesus, I can't remember what he looked like. I watch the pictures but they're sort of dead too. I sat by the window looking at the moon for a while. It's in its last quarter, and it won't be half before they take their first steps on its surface. That's tomorrow. And Petr, who wouldn't dare to go there, won't even see the event on TV. Jesus, I'm so tired. I'll try again to sleep.

A few nights later I went to Daniel.

"So," Daniel said as he sat down opposite me, "you wanted to tell me something about Paul."

"Yes. But first I would like to ask you something."

"Of course. Go ahead."

"How did you know Petr was not at the funeral?"

Daniel looked at me, surprised. "What do you mean?"

"Well, when I asked you if the one who was in love with Paul was at the funeral, you said he wasn't. But how did you know?"

Daniel looked down, his hand stroking his thigh.

"How did you know?" I repeated.

"Yes, yes, I'll tell you. Don't push me." He sighed. "Petr, or Milenec, was not at the funeral for one simple reason. He couldn't be." He paused, raised his head and looked at me. "You see, he was dead."

"But how did you know?"

He shrugged. "He was dead. Don't you understand?"

"Yes, I do understand. But how did you know he was dead? Who told you?"

His face became pale. He bent his head and hid his face in his hands.

"Did Paul tell you?"

Daniel nodded.

"Was he here the night before he died?"

"Yes," Daniel whispered.

"But why didn't you tell me? Why didn't you say? You knew I wanted to know. You knew—" Then I realized he was crying. I stopped—I was astonished—and looked at him.

"Don't cry, Daniel," I said softly and reached out for his hand. "Don't cry."

He pulled away and stared at me. "Don't cry! What do you mean?" he burst out. "You want to talk about all this old and unpleasant and sad stuff, and then you tell me not to cry! What am I supposed to do? Tell me! How do you want me to react? How?"

"I ... I don't want you to be sorry," I stuttered.

"I'm sorry now if I'm to tell you every detail, all the awful details I'd much rather forget."

He stubbed out his cigarette and lit a new one.

"I just want to know," I said hesitantly, "hat happened to my brother. That's why I'm begging you to tell me what you know, Daniel ... I know it's sad and ..."

He sighed, rose and walked to the window. "I told you already when you started this 'investigation' that you probably wouldn't like all the things you'd find. That you might even change your opinion of ... of those of us who took part ..."

"You're afraid I might not like you anymore," I interrupted.

He turned and looked at me.

"Maybe."

"But I don't understand," I said. "Why should I change? I can't judge you. I just want to know what happened. Why should I dislike you, or judge you? You didn't do anything wrong, did you? So why should I judge you?"

Daniel smiled. "That's just words. You don't know how you will react."

I shrugged. "No, I guess not. But—"

"How did you know Petr died before Paul?" Daniel broke in. "'Cause you knew even before I told you, didn't you?"

"Yes, I did. You see, I've found Paul's last diary. That's what I wanted to tell you."

Daniel seemed to run out of steam. Slowly he sank down on the couch. "I see. So, you mean Paul actually wrote in his diary not long before he died."

"Yes, he did."

"Tell me," he said. "Tell me what he wrote that last day."

I told him as fully as I could.

"Was that all?"

"Yes."

"When did he write it?"

"The twentieth," I replied. "The day before he died."

"Yes, I know that. But at what time?"

"Late, very late. It was night. He had been sleeping but woke up and started to write."

"And he didn't write anything about me?"

I shook my head.

"Are you sure?"

"Yes, I'm sure."

Daniel sighed. His hands were clasped between his legs. I could see tears in his eyes.

"What is it?" I asked. "I don't understand."

"Well, Jonas, it's something of ... a relief." He smiled a bit and wiped his eyes. "All right, I'll tell you. Since you want to know.

"You see, Paul came to me the day before he died. It was late in the afternoon. I'm not sure whether he had been home first, or if he came directly to me. And I ... I wasn't sober when he got here. I had been drinking for quite a while and I was probably quite drunk. Paul fell in through my door. He was crying and was completely devastated, asked me to hold him. We sat right here, on this couch. And he told me Petr was dead. I held him close, touched his hair, whispered comforting words. 'He's dead!

He's dead,' Paul cried. 'All the flames … and now he's dead!' And I hugged him, tried to comfort him."

Daniel was silent for a moment.

"I said, 'It'll be fine,' or something like that. 'Cause, you see, I didn't believe him. I thought maybe they had broken up, that they had had a quarrel, and Paul had rushed out, to me. I thought he meant it was over. When he said Petr was dead I thought he meant … his feelings had died. 'All the flames,' he had said. I remember it so well. But I misunderstood everything. I thought …"

He sighed and looked at me.

"Do you understand? Can you understand? I thought he was exaggerating. I thought his sorrow had made him exaggerate …"

"Go on," I said. "What happened next?"

"Well, I was tired, and drunk, and sad even before Paul got here, and I … I didn't have the strength to comfort him, I just didn't, so, half an hour later or so, I asked him to leave."

"Oh, God!" I said, but I don't think he heard me.

Daniel rubbed his eyes, and gave me a quick glance. "Did you hear that?" he said. "*I asked him to leave!* Can you imagine? I thought it was all some lovers' quarrel, or something like that, so I asked him to leave. And Paul left. For the very last time."

I couldn't think of anything to say. I just sat there on the couch, looking at Daniel. He leaned back in his chair, his eyes closed. Suddenly I thought he looked old. His face was worn and haggard, and I had always thought he made a youthful impression, as if he was caught in some strange youth zone. But now it looked as if the years had caught up with him.

"When did you find out?"

He shivered and opened his eyes. "What did you say?"

"When did you realize it was true? That Petr really had died?"

"The next day. I didn't wake up until half past twelve. And I didn't even bother to get my morning paper. Only hours later I picked it up. And just as I was starting to read it, Sara called and told me what had happened to Paul.

"I dropped the paper, and although I was very tense while she was telling me about Paul's death, I couldn't avoid reading that newspaper headline over and over. I can still see it clearly: Violent fire in Saltvik claims victims. I still don't understand it. I mean, I was completely shocked by what Sara told me—I could repeat what she said word for word—but still my bloody hang-overed head managed to read that headline, over and over."

"How horrible!" I whispered.

Daniel stared at me.

"What did the article say?" I asked after a while.

"The article? I don't think I ever read it. Just that headline. Over and over."

"So you still knew Petr was ..."

He nodded.

"But, I still don't understand how—"

"How I could be so bloody stupid as to ask Paul to leave?" Daniel interrupted angrily.

His voice frightened me.

"No!" I burst out. And then suddenly I realized, "Oh, so that's it! You think I'll hate you 'cause you asked him to go."

"Yes, of course," he replied sharply.

"I can understand your feeling bad about asking Paul to leave," I started slowly, "but I don't see how you could think I

124

would hate you for it. You told me yourself you were sad and tired, and drunk. And that you thought Paul was exaggerating. So you didn't do anything wrong. It was just a misunderstanding."

"A misunderstanding?" Daniel shouted. "Some bloody misunderstanding! I didn't understand any word he said. Instead, I read in something completely different and sent him away."

Now I was really getting frightened.

"You didn't *send him* away. You told me yourself that you asked—"

"What does it matter if I sent him away or asked him to leave? If I had listened to him he would never have ..." He didn't finish the sentence.

My hands were shaking. I pushed them hard against my legs so that Daniel wouldn't notice.

"Killed himself, you mean?"

He nodded silently. And I barely dared to ask my next question: "Do you really think Paul killed himself?"

"I don't know," Daniel whispered. "Sometimes I think he did, and then I feel ..."

"Guilty," I suggested.

"Yes. But sometimes, or most of the time, I believe it was an accident. He used to dream a bit. Then you had to repeat his name over and over before he noticed."

"I know."

"But my guilt is there somewhere, in my putting Paul off that very last night of his life. That is what he accuses me of in my nightmares. That I didn't listen to him, that I didn't help him. That I was so ... It was the bloody alcohol. I couldn't understand what he said. How could I have been so—"

"But you're exaggerating," I interrupted. "You *misunderstood* what he said. You can't be judged for that. And I don't think Paul killed himself. I'm sure he didn't."

Daniel looked at me in wonder. "What makes you think it wasn't suicide?"

"I just don't believe it was. He was sad, of course. He must have been grieving terribly. But still he wrote in his diary that he was going to tell Mother and Father about Petr. He just needed to wait for a while. He needed to pull himself together after that terrible accident. But he wanted to tell them about Petr. And, by the way, he wrote about the landing on the moon as well. He was absolutely thrilled by the idea they were going to land on the moon. He wrote about it all the time. Even that last day he wrote about the landing on the moon. I don't think he would have wanted to miss that event."

Daniel nodded. "Yes, that's true. I haven't thought about it. He did actually speak a lot about the moon landing. Yes, I haven't thought about that. I remember the satellite telecast. I remember the camera angle when Neil Armstrong, or whoever it was, stepped down from the ladder and reached the moon surface. He—"

"Well, there you are," I interrupted. "While you were watching television you were just as close to forgetting a friend as Paul was when he went for his forest walk."

"What do you mean?"

"I mean, you're not completely filled with sorrow or grief even the first day after a friend's death. You could, although you were shocked and saddened by Paul's death, watch the TV news, and Paul could, in spite of the fact he had lost his best friend the day before, go for a forest walk. That's what I mean. The sorrow isn't constant even the first day. It comes and goes, like waves on the shore. There may be shorter intervals between some waves, but, still, you get a break before the next one. And during that break you may have time to watch TV or go for a walk in the woods. It's almost 'as usual,' in the breaks. Do you see what I mean?"

"Yes, I do. And it's probably like that, that the sorrow seems to go away for a moment. But it's also true that sorrow has its own life, and that you can nourish your sorrow with your thoughts. And there's a risk that your thoughts get caught up in the sorrow, making it more or less constant. Perhaps it will even come to control you, and then you can't get away."

"Yes, I see what you mean," I said, "but I don't think Paul was possessed by sorrow. You can tell from his diary that he was thinking of other things as well. He wanted to speak about Petr. Not only of his death, but also about Petr as a person, as a ... lover. But he didn't have the strength at that time. And, as I told you, he wrote about the landing on the moon. So I don't think he committed suicide, and I definitely don't think he's accusing you of anything. He knew you, Daniel. That's why he came to you for comfort. Which you tried to give him. And that was actually all you could do, wasn't it? You couldn't bring Petr back to life. All you could do was comfort Paul by saying those things you say when someone is sad. You can't change what has happened, even if you'd like to."

"Yes," Daniel said, after a while. "I guess you're right. And I do regard Paul's death as an accident most of the time. It's just, sometimes, when I'm feeling low, I get to thinking he killed himself."

"That's just what I mean," I said. "When you're feeling sad and low you nourish your sorrow over the loss of Paul with your thoughts about your, perhaps, having had something to do with his death. And that's when the sorrow lives its own life, that's when the sorrow grows stronger than you."

"Yes," Daniel managed.

We were silent for quite a long while. I could see he was still unhappy, but I also felt I had reached him, and that his sadness wasn't quite as intense as before. I had nothing more to say. I had done all I could. I had mixed my own thoughts and speculations with quotes from my mother and my father. Through all my childhood I had heard their conversations about Paul, about the sorrow they felt after his death. You could, perhaps, say I grew up in a small world of sorrow. Perhaps I am even the fruit of an early stage in my parents' mourning, the result of their mutual efforts to carry on. And now I had at least tried to help Daniel in *his* mourning.

"I think I'd like to go home soon."

"Of course," said Daniel, looking up. "It's getting late."

He rose and walked to the window.

"I'm sorry if I frightened you, but I was so upset. I like you, that's what I want you to know. And I like talking with you. But I think we should stop talking about Paul and Petr. We only get depressed. I don't mean we should stop talking about them in every way, but we should not continue to go over the sad things that happened in their lives."

"But everything in Paul's life wasn't sorrowful," I said. "The only sad thing, I mean *really* sad thing that happened to him, as far as I know, was when Petr died. The other sad things happened in *your* life, and in the lives of my mother and father. You all were stricken by grief. Paul's death was the cause of it, and by talking about what happened to him, we also talk about your sorrow, and so it is somewhat dissipated. So, I think we should talk about Paul."

"Well, perhaps."

17

Spring arrived, then summer. I had started to write about you, Paul. About you and Petr. But it was much more difficult than I had expected. Several times I threw away full pages, because they didn't turn out the way I wanted them to. Or, rather, the way I thought things had happened. Every time, I started with your diary and with what my parents and Daniel had told me, but my romanticized story was either too dramatic or too close to sentimentality. So I erased, and rewrote, or tore up. I was obsessed by the thought of writing about you, Paul, about what really had happened. At night, after I had gone to bed, I thought intensely of you, hoping my thoughts would make you appear in my dreams. But I didn't dream of you.

I was writing about the Walpurgis Night that Paul and Petr celebrated together when there was a knock on my door. I put the diary in the drawer of my desk before answering.

It was Mother.

"Hi. What are you doing?"

"Just writing," I replied.

"I see. I was just going to ask you if you're going to go swimming tomorrow."

"I'm not sure. I guess so. Why?"

"Well, it's the twenty-first," Mother replied. "Stefan and I are planning to visit the cemetery and put fresh flowers on Paul's grave. I thought maybe you could come with us."

"Yes, I would like to," I answered. "When are you going?"

"I don't know. We haven't got any other plans. Were you thinking of swimming?"

I nodded.

"We can bring our swim clothes and go together to the shore. After the cemetery. Wouldn't that be nice? We don't do that much together anymore, the three of us."

"Sure. That would be nice."

The stone was almost quadrate, small and black. Almost insignificant.

PAUL LUNDBERG
15 years
OSKARSHAMN

No year of birth. No year of death. Still, it was my brother's grave.

"But there're flowers here already," my mother burst out, surprised. "Someone must have put them here today. The water's up to the edge."

"Perhaps it was Grandma," said Father as he squatted down in front of the stone, "or your parents."

"No, I don't think so. They would have told us if they were coming this way, don't you think?"

"It might be Daniel," I suggested.

"Yes, maybe."

Father planted the flower Mother had brought, stood up and brushed the soil from his hands.

"It's eighteen years since he died," Mother murmured, "yet it seems so recent. As if it happened yesterday. Don't you agree, Stefan?"

We were lying on a huge rock, sunbathing.

"Oh, I can't stand this anymore," Mother said, and got up. "It's just too hot. I have to take a dip. Are you coming?"

"Later," said Father.

"Yes, later," I said and closed my eyes and listened to all the sounds surrounding us: children laughing and screaming, radios pouring out some summer program. From far away I could hear the rattling of a boat engine. And I thought of Paul and Petr's last day together.

"Hey!"

"What?"

"Do you know if there's any Czech family living in town?"

Father opened his eyes for a moment. "A Czech family? I guess so. The woman who used to work at the Saga Theater came from Czechoslovakia. What's her name? Ludmila, I think. She's married to one of my schoolmates."

"Yes, but I mean a Czech *family*," I said.

He thought for a moment. "Well, not that I know of. At least not anymore."

"What do you mean?"

"There was a Czech man working at the harbor several years

ago. Adam was his name. He and his family came from Czechoslovakia. From Prague, I believe."

"Do you remember his last name?"

"Not really. He had a difficult name to pronounce. Sha … Sho … Shore … That's it. Shorely. But it wasn't pronounced like that. I never learned to say it right. We called him Adam most of the time. But it was Shorely. Adam Shorely."

Mother came back from the water. She sat down next to Father and started to dry her hair.

"Who are you talking about?" she asked.

"Adam Shorely," Father replied. "Do you remember him?"

"No, not really. But I do recognize the name."

Father sat up. "But you must remember him. He was a kind of lanky guy, and he always wore a cap." Then his voice changed. "It was his house that burned down in Saltvik. Don't you remember? Someone died. But Adam wasn't hurt. You must remember. He was working at the harbor. And after the fire they moved to Kalmar."

"Yes," Mother hesitated, "I think I remember."

I had began to feel cold. *P.S.* That's how Petr had ended his letters. And I had wondered why he never wrote any postscript.

"When did this happen?" I asked, trying not to sound too interested.

Father thought for a while. "Well, it was long ago. It must have been before you were born." He turned to Mother. "I think it was in 1969."

I sat up and put the towel over my shoulders.

"The same year Paul died," I said in a low voice.

"Yes, the same year."

"Did you know him?"

"Adam? No, I can't say I did. We said 'hello' when we met at the harbor. But since we never worked together …"

It took a while before I dared to continue.

"You said his house burned down."

"Yes."

"Was it … Did it happen in the summer? At the time of Paul's death?"

"Yes, I told you."

"Tell me more."

He looked curiously at me.

"Well, there's not much more to tell, really. I don't remember why it started to burn in the first place. But they weren't at home when it started. Or … No. It was Adam who wasn't there. He came later. It must have been an explosive fire, I guess, since no one had time to get out."

I could feel my mother watching me, but I didn't dare turn and meet her eyes.

"Go on," I said.

"The house was almost completely in flames when the firemen got there. All they could do was to be sure the fire didn't spread. But they couldn't save the house."

"And when did they find him?" I asked in a tense voice.

Now both my parents were staring at me.

"Who?" my father asked.

I glanced at my mother. She looked frightened.

"He … who died," I stuttered.

"You're not listening to me," my father said, irritated. "Adam didn't die. But his wife did."

"But the son, he died too," I persisted.

"No, he survived. But he had severe—"

"Enough! You must end this gruesome conversation," Mother interrupted. "It's absolutely ... gruesome sitting here telling details of an accident that happened ages ago." She stared at me. "What are you up to, Jonas? Why are you so interested in that family? You don't know anything about them. You don't know them. It happened long before you were even born.

"And you," she continued, turning to my father, "why are you telling him all these horrid details? Why?"

I could feel tears coming.

"I'm sorry," I whispered, and quickly stood up.

The water was ice-cold when I dived in.

18

There was a knock on my door.

"Yes?"

"It's only me," said Mother as she came in.

I was in bed with my arms around my pillow.

"Dinner's ready soon," she said. "Are you hungry?"

"I guess."

Silence.

"What are you up to, Jonas?" she asked.

I buried my face in the pillow.

"Hey! You can tell me, can't you?"

And I started to cry.

Mother took my hands in hers.

"Easy now, easy," she whispered. "You'll feel better if you tell me, don't you think?" She leaned close and whispered in my ear, "Certainly this pillowcase can be washed, but I don't know how many salty tears it can stand."

"Don't joke! This is not a joking matter."

"Oh, I'm sorry! I didn't mean to … Listen, Jonas, I do understand this is serious, otherwise you'd never act this way, but I can't help you unless you tell me what it's all about."

I wanted to tell her everything, but I didn't believe I could. And I didn't want to lie to her.

"I've dreamed some … some horrible things lately."

She was still holding my hands.

"I'm not sure, but some of my dreams have been almost real. About real things. And I've learned about some things that have happened. Real things, I mean. Things that have actually happened. I've dreamed about these things, these horrible things. And although I don't know the people I dream about, it's like I'm getting to know them, or getting to know about them. 'Cause you see, some of them are dead."

"You mean, you've dreamed about that Czech family?"

"Yes."

"And you have dreamed about the house that burned down, where somebody died."

I nodded. "Yes, but the dreams were somewhat different from what Father told me."

Mother was silent for a moment, looking out the window. Then she turned toward me. A curl of hair fell over her forehead. She had tears in her eyes.

"Well, Jonas," she said, "I know dreams, nightmares, can be really horrible at times. No matter whether they are real or just confused thoughts in our sleep. Perhaps you sleep too little— you do read a lot at night—and if you don't get enough sleep, you get touchy about whatever happens, or whatever you dream. Maybe it would be better if you tried to sleep more."

"Yes, maybe."

"You have to forgive me for bursting out like that at the sea-shore," she said, "but I thought I'd lose my mind listening to you dwelling on all those details of that terrible fire."

"That's all right. I was almost losing my mind too," I said. "Do you remember that family?"

"Yes. I thought about them in the car. I do remember them. I met her, the wife, once at the hospital. She had lost her way, and I helped her find the right ward. And I remember Adam too, but only vaguely."

"What about the son? Do you remember him?"

She shook her head. "No, I don't remember ever seeing him. I just remember what the newspaper said about him. He had some rather severe injuries from the fire and was unconscious at the hospital for some time. I remember wondering if he knew his mother was dead."

I looked at her, astonished. "When did you read about him?"

"It was in the paper the day after the fire," she replied, "the day Paul died."

"And you remember? Although it was the same day Paul died, you remember an article about some other family? Some other boy?"

"Well, yes. It's probably because of that. I think I remember everything that happened that day."

"Can you ..."

"What?"

"Can you remember his name? The other boy's name?"

She thought for a while.

"Yes. He was called Peter. No, wait ... Petr! That's it. Petr." And suddenly she stiffened.

"What is it?" I asked, and swallowed.

"I just remembered something," she said. "I believe Paul knew a Czech boy who was called Petr. Yes, it was the same name, and now I suddenly have the feeling it was the same boy ... What if it was the same boy? The one who lost his mother, and the one who knew Paul."

I swallowed once more. "It's hardly likely," I said. "Petr is probably a very common name, don't you think? Just like Peter is a very common name here."

Mother nodded. "Yes, of course. That's probably the case. Anyway, it really doesn't matter anymore, does it?"

"No. It doesn't matter at all," I replied. "Not now."

19

A brass plate with the inscription Editorial Office told me I was right. I knocked on the door.

"Come in!"

A woman was standing with her back toward me as I entered the room. She turned around and smiled.

"Hello! Can I help you?"

"I'd like to look at an old newspaper," I replied.

"I see. How old? From what date, I mean."

"July 21, 1969."

She giggled. "Oops! That's quite a long time ago. I guess you weren't even thought of back then."

"No," I replied. "I wasn't."

"Well, of course you can look. Just wait a second and I'll get the key."

She pulled out an enormous cloth-covered book from one of the many shelves.

"Yes, here we are," she said, and pointed to the label. "This volume has the editions of July 1969. I'll put it here on the desk for you. Is that okay?"

"Yes, thanks."

She pointed toward the other end of the room.

"I have some articles to copy," she said. "I'll be over there. Just tell me when you've finished. Or if you need any help."

There was quite a lot about the coming landing on the moon, but I didn't look at the grayish satellite photographs. On the fourth page I found the headline Daniel had been reading over and over again:

VIOLENT FIRE IN SALTVIK CLAIMS VICTIMS.

I whooped, and glanced toward the other end of the room. I could barely see the woman behind the dusty pane of glass. Then I started to read:

A violent fire destroyed a detached house in Saltvik yesterday afternoon. A woman in her 50's was killed while her 16-year-old son escaped with injuries from the fire. The husband was not at home when the fire started. Although the fire brigade and the ambulance were at the scene quickly the heavy buildup of smoke made it impossible to save the house. The woman was already dead when she was found, while the 16-year-old boy showed signs of life. The boy was brought to the hospital in Västervik where his injuries were considered not serious. The violent fire threatened to spread to buildings nearby. Only around 10 p.m. did the firemen manage to put it out. The house was completely destroyed. It is still not known what caused the fire, but it could have been an electric flashover. The husband is in shock and is still in the hospital.

Confused and shaken, I turned the pages. I had hoped to find Petr's surname in print. I knew neither how it was pronounced nor how it was spelled. Maybe I would find the announcement of his mother's death farther on.

But my eyes were caught by something else.

BOY KILLED IN TRAIN ACCIDENT.

"Jesus!" I whispered. I hadn't even thought about that. I hadn't expected to find an article on Paul's death. On my brother's death.

A 15-year-old boy from Döderhult outside Oskarshamn was killed when he was hit by the train Monday afternoon. The accident happened just after a curve some 5 kilometers west of Oskarshamn. The boy did not notice the signals from the engineer, who never had the chance to stop the train. The boy was said to be out on a walk in the forest. He knew the area quite well and was aware of the frequent use of the track. He was killed instantly.

That was all. A short article about my brother's death.

"Jesus!" I whispered once more. Petr and Paul—Milenec and Princi—were no more than a "16-year-old son" and "a 15-year-old boy." There are certainly many ways in which you can describe an event. Or describe a person who has lived and loved, cried and laughed. A person who has lived and died—a person just like you or me—can have his or her entire life reduced to a few short lines in a newspaper, which rapidly loses its current interest before it turns yellow and is thrown away, or is hidden in some dusty dark archive.

I didn't recognize my brother and his friend in those brief articles.

"Did you find what you were looking for?"

Quickly, I turned around.

"Oh, I'm sorry," said the woman. "Did I frighten you? I'm so sorry."

I murmured something.

"Well, did you find what you were looking for?" she repeated.

I nodded.

She took off her glasses and looked at me. Her eyes were a strange blue color. "May I ask what you were looking for?"

"Yes. Yes, of course," I replied and pointed to the article.

She put her glasses back on and read it.

"So," she said, "how come you were looking for this particular article? You weren't even born then."

"It was my brother," I explained. "He died the year before I was born. Seventeen months before I was born."

"I see," she said warmly, "that's sad. So you never had the chance to know him, did you?"

I shook my head.

"What was his name?"

"It was Paul. Paul Lundberg."

"Yes, of course. You're Sara Lundberg's son, aren't you? I should have guessed. You look a lot like her."

"You know my mother?"

"Yes. Well, I knew her when I was young. We were in school together, Sara and I. But I haven't seen her for ages. I remember how sad I was for Sara when I read the announcement of your brother's death. It must have been terrible for her. And for your father, too. I was so happy when I heard she had had another son. And here you are, right before me. The second son."

"Yes."

"My name's Agneta. Agneta Carlsson. Please remember me to your mother."

"Yes, I will," I said. "By the way, that announcement ... about Paul. When was that?"

She leaned over the bound newspapers.

"Let's see," she said, and carefully browsed through the fragile pages. "That shouldn't be too hard to find. Let's see ... No, it doesn't seem to be here."

She closed the book and took down the next volume from the shelf. She searched for a short while, then stopped and pointed with a ringed finger.

I went closer and leaned over the page. And so I read the announcement of my brother's death.

And after your name—*a star and a cross*—and after your parents' and my parents' names—*Sara and Stefan*—and after the nameless group of people who knew you—*relatives and friends*—someone had chosen a line from a poem in an attempt to explain to you and to all of us why you had been taken away from us so early:

Eternity is in love with the productions of time.

I read the words once again, and then again.

Eternity is in love with the productions of time.

I thought about the words and found that I liked them. They fitted in the picture I had made of what had happened. It was the only reasonable explanation. Every other explanation only gave me more thoughts, other questions. This was in some way the best explanation. Sufficient.

Eternity is in love with the productions of time.

The woman by my side gently touched my arm. "William Blake," she said.

"Sorry?"

"It was William Blake who wrote that line. I recognize it. We had a boy in our class who tried to make us read Blake. I don't think he managed to persuade anyone. But I do remember that line. It's so beautiful."

"Yes, it is."

I returned to the page, and suddenly I saw how Petr spelled his name:

Our beloved
Daniela Shořelá
* 28 April 1924   † 20 July 1969
Adam & Petr Shořely
Tvůj anděl je s tebou

"Agneta!" my mother burst out when I told her of my visit to the editorial office. "That's really nice. I haven't seen her for ages."

"I read the announcement of Paul's death," I continued.

"You did? Haven't you read it before?"

I shook my head.

"Oh, you haven't. There's a clipping somewhere. I believe it's in one of the drawers in our bedroom. Together with some short article on … on the accident."

"Yes, I saw that article as well," I said. "It was so short. I wasn't looking for it, but when I found it and read it, I thought it was so paltry. Almost nothing. But I did like that poetry line."

"What poetry line?"

"The one in the announcement. 'Eternity is in love with the productions of time.' Agneta told me it was written by William Blake."

"Yes, that's right. So, she recognized it?"

"Yes," I replied and told her what Agneta had told me.

Mother smiled. "Yes, I remember that line too," she said. "I could almost say it has followed me. It's one of those sentences that turns up in your thoughts every now and then. Like some strange motto. Like some magic rigmarole."

"Did you meet that guy?"

"What guy?"

"The one in Agneta's class. The one who read Blake."

Mother laughed. "Yes, you can definitely say I've met him."

"What's so funny?"

"You've met him too, Jonas. You see, it was Daniel."

"Hey, Jonas," Mother said, sometime later, "I have a feeling you're still working on that 'crossword.' Is that so? The one you were working on a couple of years ago. When you started to ask us things, Daniel and me. You thought maybe we could help you."

I nodded.

"I think you should stop. It seems like it's a burden for you, and 'crosswords' should be entertaining, shouldn't they? If you stop this, you will probably sleep a lot better, and maybe you will be free from those horrid nightmares."

"Yes, maybe," I replied. "But there's only one word left, and after that, the crossword is done, and my nightmares will be gone."

"You really think so?"

"Yes, I really do."

20

That evening I wrote to Petr Shořely. After my visit to the editorial office I went to the Telecom shop. I don't remember how many telephone directories I searched through before I found his name. And when I did, I found it in the directory for my own hometown and its surroundings. "Shorely, Petr," I read. There were no diacritical marks, and the name was not followed by a title. But there was the address to a street in Påskallavik, a small community some twenty kilometers south of town. I felt absolutely happy when I found it, and immediately decided to write him.

I told him who I was and why I was contacting him. "I would like to meet you. Soon. Preferably before school starts. There's so much I want to ask you. And there are things I would like to show you. Please answer soon."

Only after I had sealed the envelope and put on a stamp, did I began to feel somewhat reluctant.

"Are you going out now?" my father asked, surprised. "It's almost midnight."

"I know," I said, "but I want to put this in the mailbox."

"It won't go any faster if you do that tonight," said he. "They won't empty the box until tomorrow afternoon."

"I know, but I want to mail this now."

That night I dreamed about my brother.

He was sitting on the side of the bed. He leaned over me and whispered my name.

"Yes?"

"Come with me," said Paul. "All the stars are out tonight."

He took my hand and led me out into the night. The stars glittered stronger than ever before. They seemed to float just over the roofs and the treetops.

"Can you see this, Jonas?" Paul asked, and made a gesture toward the sky.

"Yes," I replied. "Now I see."

"Do you know what you see?"

I shook my head.

"It's Eternity's fireworks. Eternal fireworks that constantly enchant us. Fireworks we always have above our heads, although we cannot always see them. It's Eternity's fireworks."

"But what is Eternity?" I wondered.

Paul didn't answer. He smiled.

"Is it a living thing?" I asked. "Or a force? Or is it maybe a god?"

He shook his head. "No, Eternity is not a living thing, nor is it a god. Perhaps it is a force. Eternity is our thoughts and wishes."

"But why was Eternity in love with you?"

"Eternity is in love with all things captured by time. That includes you too, Jonas. Eternity sees you. Sees your eyes. But your eyes are caught in time. Eternity doesn't know about time. Eternity moves far beyond time and therefore cannot see through your eyes. That is why Eternity is in love with you and everyone else who lives within time."

"But shouldn't I be with you, then?"

"You'll be here someday. In time. But there's no hurry. Eternity is never in a hurry. That's in its nature."

"But if Eternity is never in a hurry, how come you died so young?"

Paul shrugged, and smiled. "Well, it just happened," he replied. "I was just standing there thinking of Eternity and the stars and being in love, and ..."

"And what about Petr?"

Paul caressed my cheek.

"Petr," he whispered. "Můj bratře."

21

The summer holiday was over and school had started without any message from Petr. For a while I thought about writing him another letter, but I never did. I had nothing else to tell him. It would only have been a repetition of my first letter.

"Is something bothering you?" my mother asked me one day.

"Well, not really."

She searched my face. "Is it the 'crossword'?"

I couldn't help but smile. "Yes, in a way. But it's not only that."

"No? Do you want to talk about it?"

I shook my head.

"Will you tell me everything when this is over?"

I looked at her. "Perhaps," I replied. "I'm not sure. Perhaps."

I was lying in bed. Beside me—on my bedside table—was the blue Austin. I reached out for it, turned the red plastic steering wheel, and watched the front wheels move. Back and forth, back and forth. Behind the scratched windscreen I could dimly see two plastic figures. I held the car closer to me. It was still impossible to see their faces. And I remembered that when I was small I sometimes wondered whether the figures were happy or sad.

And so I thought about Petr.

And so I made up my mind.

Mother was sitting at the kitchen table.

"You want some coffee?" she asked. "There's enough for you too."

I poured a cup and sat down opposite her.

"You know, Mum," I began after a while, "I've been thinking about visiting a friend this weekend."

"Oh? Who?"

"A boy from school," I lied. "He lives in Påskallavik. I'm thinking about taking the first bus. On Saturday morning, I mean."

"Will you stay overnight?"

Her question took me by surprise. I hadn't really thought about it that much. But I believe I managed to keep my face fairly calm and ordinary.

"I'm not sure," I replied. "We haven't talked about it. It depends on whether we'll be late or not."

"So, what are you going to do?"

I shrugged. "Nothing special. We'll just be talking, I guess. Listening to records and such."

"That sounds nice," said Mother. "I hope you will have a nice time."

22

The bus driver turned and waved to me.

"This is it."

"Thanks a lot," I said and stood up.

The bus stopped. The doors opened, and I got off.

I put down my bag and looked around. In a garden some hundred meters from the bus stop stood an enormous glass statue, a shimmering blue human form. Almost the same color as my Austin, I thought. A blue glass boy.

I took the map out of my bag. The garden with the glass statue was my objective. I looked at the map, counting the cross-streets. Then I looked up and started to walk.

It was a small wooden house in a shady garden. It looked like a summerhouse.

I stopped outside the gate. The scrollworked five on the mailbox told me I was right. My hand shook as I opened the gate.

It felt unreal. I read the letters on the nameplate beside the doorbell over and over. For a long time I just stood there, not daring to ring.

The sound of a barking dog broke the spell. I turned around. An old woman on the other side of the street was looking at me.

Her fat dog was barking and straining at its leash.

I turned back and rang the doorbell.

Nothing happened.

I rang again. And the dog barked.

Just as I was going to ring for the third time, the door opened partway and Petr's dark eyes were glaring at me.

Then, quick as lightning, his face changed. He seemed shocked.

"Hello," I said quietly.

"Oh, God!" sighed Petr.

The fat dog across the street barked angrily.

Petr glanced at the lady and the dog, then said, "Come in!" and opened the door for me. Only then did I see he was almost naked. He had a towel wrapped around his loins.

I stared, amazed at his body. A huge mark—stretching from his left hip, over his chest, and almost up to his right nipple—looked like the giant imprint of a hand. And the strangely colored skin had a soft glimmer, almost like silk.

Petr quickly closed the door and stared at me.

"It's me, Jonas," I stuttered. "Paul's brother."

Petr backed away a step and muttered something that sounded like *crucifix*.

"I was just going to have a shower. I was …" He didn't finish the sentence.

"Am I disturbing you?" was all I could think of.

And he laughed. "Disturbing me? I really don't know. Not yet."

I tried not to look at the strange mark.

Petr sighed. "I'm sorry. I was absolutely astonished when I saw you. I had never expected to— Well, come on in! You can hang your jacket here. And you can sit in the living room while I take a shower."

I nodded, embarrassed.

Petr led me into the living room.

"Play some music, if you like," he said, pointing to the stereo. "I'll be back soon."

It still felt unreal. I was moving around in Petr's living room, looking at his paintings and knickknacks, reading the titles of his books, and going through his recordings. As if I belonged there, as if it were some familiar place. Or as if I were someone else.

I picked a record at random and was suddenly surrounded by an odd choir. Strange words in a magic tune. And my hands stopped shaking.

I sat down on the couch and closed my eyes.

"Jonas?"

I twitched.

Petr was standing on the other side of the low table. I hadn't heard him come in. But now he was there. *Petr je tady.*

"Did I frighten you?"

"No, not at all."

I was watching him while he was speaking and I recognized him from the pictures in my brother's photo albums. His face was a bit rounder than it had been when Paul took pictures of him down by the bay. But his profile was the same. And the dark eyes.

"You will have to excuse me, but I really had a shock when I opened the door."

"Did you think I was Paul?"

Petr smiled, and the smile was the same as in the photos. "No. I didn't. I could see it was you, but I had hardly expected you to show up here. I really hadn't."

I looked away.

Petr went over to the stereo and turned down the volume.

"How long will you stay? I mean, are you … are you leaving soon?"

"I'm not sure," I murmured. "I just wanted to see you."

He looked at me for a moment, then he smiled. "Well, Jonas, I was supposed to meet a working mate in an hour or so, but I can call him and tell him I can't come. Will that be okay? I mean, then we'll have some time on our own, you and me."

I just nodded.

Petr laughed and sat down by my side. "Don't look so miserable," he said. "I'm not dangerous. And I'm not at all angry, if that's what you think. I was just so amazed when I saw you."

He reached out his hand and touched my arm. "I really wanted to answer your letter, but I didn't know what to say. You wrote you wanted to talk about your brother. That you wanted to learn more about him. But I wasn't really sure that I wanted to talk about Paul. You must understand that it's hard for me. It's still hard to think about him. But, we can give it a try. Since you're here."

23

After we had coffee, Petr showed me his small house. Here and there we stopped and Petr told me something or other about the painting or whatever it was we were looking at. In his study there were two oval-framed photos.

"These are my parents."

"Adam and Daniela," I said.

Petr laughed. "How did you know?"

"I read it somewhere."

Petr stared at me. Then suddenly he smiled. "I see. I'm beginning to understand."

I smiled back, slightly embarrassed.

"You have read Paul's diary, haven't you?"

I nodded. And Petr laughed again, his dark eyes glittering. Then his face changed.

"Jesus, you do look like him," he whispered.

I looked down at the floor, not knowing how to respond.

"I'm sorry. I didn't mean to …" Petr said.

We were sitting side by side on the couch in Petr's living room. I had taken out the photographs that I had found in Paul's treasure box and showed them to him. I had told him about my brother, how my image of him had changed over the years, and I had told him about how I found the diary and the pictures.

I was starting to feel more relaxed.

"It's just like Sherlock Holmes," Petr said. "When did all this happen?"

"It was rather long ago," I replied, and tried to remember. "No, perhaps not that long ago. First I found the photographs, and later the diary."

"I see. And you didn't know of my existence until you found the diary, did you?"

I was a bit confused by his question. "Well, not really."

"That's a strange answer. What do you mean?"

I cleared my throat and coughed a little to gain some time. But although I hesitated I knew I didn't want to lie—I *couldn't* lie—to Petr. I didn't even want to make a euphemism of the truth.

"Well, it was when I first read Paul's diary that I found any information about you. But you asked me if the diary told me of your existence, didn't you?"

He nodded and looked at me in wonder.

"That's not what I learned," I continued. "I only learned that you *had* existed. Because, you see, Paul thought you died when the house burned down."

I saw Petr turn pale. He bent forward, buried his face in his hands, and mumbled something. For a while all I could do was wait. But then I broke the silence:

"Do you want me to tell you? Why Paul thought you were dead?"

"Yes, do."

"Paul waited for you on the beach, but since you took so long, he decided to bike over to your house. He arrived soon after the fire brigade and the ambulance. And he saw a badly burned body on a stretcher. The paramedics were covering the body just as Paul noticed it, but he could still see the feet sticking out from under the cover. He could clearly see your red gym shoes, Petr."

"Oh my God!" Petr whispered. He was in tears, and once again he murmured a word that sounded like *crucifix*.

"It wasn't *me* lying on the stretcher," he said in a voice close to crying, "it was my mother. She must have had her gym shoes on. They were just like mine. But it wasn't me. I was on the way to the hospital by the time they found her. She was upstairs. Why didn't he ask the rescuers? They could have told him. They could have explained … Oh, God! He thought I was dead …"

We were silent for a moment. I wanted to say something comforting but couldn't find the words. Instead, I asked him to tell me about the fire.

"The house was all in flames," he began. "Afterwards, at the hospital, I was told a neighbor had called the fire brigade, but they hadn't arrived when I got there. I hadn't realized the house was burning until I got close on my bike, and when I saw the flames I lost my balance. I drove straight into a stone or a tree stump or something, and fell. I sprained my ankle and could hardly walk. It's almost comic when you think about my more or less jumping on one leg up to the house. I knew Mum was upstairs, and I was trying to save her. It was all dark inside because of the smoke, and I fell at the stairs. I must have hit my head and passed out. The next thing I remember is waking up in the hospital."

"When did you know your mother was dead?"

"In the evening. My father and a psychologist came to my room and told me. But I had already feared the worst. They just confirmed what I was thinking."

Petr leaned back on the couch and ran his fingers through his hair.

"And what about Paul? When did you find out that he had died?"

"Oh, that was a couple of days later. I was still in the special ward. My father had read about the accident. And then, I believe, one of his working mates told him who the dead boy was. That it was Paul who had died."

"Jesus, it's so awful," I whispered. "It means you lost two of your closest …"

"Yes," Petr sighed, "it was terrible, absolutely terrible."

Petr was looking at the picture of Paul coming out of the bathroom.

"Was it taken at your place?" I asked.

"Yes. I took it in the morning after our first night together. Oh God, I was so in love with him. I thought he was just wonderful. He was beautiful and … magical."

"Like a *Princi*."

Petr laughed. "Yes, like a Princi." And now his eyes were wet again. "You seem to know everything about the two of us, don't you?"

I shrugged.

Petr touched my cheek. "I had a shock the first time I saw you. I thought you looked so much like him. It was almost like seeing

Paul again. But now, when you're close, I can see you're not that much alike. More like ordinary brothers."

"What do you mean? Have you seen me before?"

"Yes. This summer. At the cemetery. I was—"

"So it was you who put the flowers on Paul's grave."

Petr nodded. "Yes, it was me. I've visited his grave a couple of times when I've been in the neighborhood. But now, this summer, I had decided to visit the grave on the anniversary of Paul's death." He laughed. "I felt caught when I saw you coming into the churchyard. Like I was doing something illegal."

"You saw us coming?"

"Yes, just as I stood up, I saw you open the gate. For a moment I just stared at you. Then I turned and went out through the other gate. I didn't want to be seen. I didn't … I didn't want to see you."

We kept talking for hours, Petr and I. About Paul.

He added more to the things I already knew, and he told me a lot I didn't know.

"Did Paul speak Czech? I mean, so he could actually speak the language?"

Petr shook his head. "No. He just learned some words and phrases. Things I taught him. I always thought he sounded like a child when he said anything in Czech. It wasn't his pronunciation, not at all. But he spoke like a child. Only much later I realized it was because of my own Czech. Paul was just imitating me. I was just a child when we moved from Prague. First to Hamburg, and then to Sweden. And I didn't speak Czech that often once we got here. Mum and Dad wanted to learn Swedish as soon as possible. And so my knowledge of Czech got less. I guess you could say my language remained at a childish level. But I didn't realize how childish it sounded until I heard Paul speak the words I had taught him. Do you see what I mean?"

"Yes, I think I do," I replied, and inadvertently yawned.

Petr touched my cheek. "Poor thing," he whispered. "We've been sitting here talking for hours. Perhaps we could save the rest of the story till later. If you're starting to get bored."

"No, I'm not," I said and stretched. "I just feel a bit tired. Besides, there's one thing I have to ask you."

"Really?" Petr giggled. "I believe you've been asking me questions all along."

"Yes, I know, but I've been waiting to ask you this particular question. The other ones just came at random."

"So what's the question?"

"Well, I wonder what happened at ten past twelve on Friday, September 20, 1968."

At first he just stared at me. Then his eyes started to glitter and he laughed. "Are you crazy? You think I'm some kind of living computer, don't you!"

"Yes, actually I do," I said, laughing too. "In a way …"

"Well, let's see … Let me think. You said September 20, 1968?"

"Yes."

"And that was a Friday?"

"Yes. And the time was twelve-ten."

"Well, for one thing, it was the day before my birthday. So it must have been my last day as a fourteen-year-old …

"I see," he said quietly. "I know what you mean. It was when I saw Paul for the first time."

"Yes."

"Outside the school refectory. I haven't thought about that for ages. He was looking at something lying on the ground. He was so beautiful."

"I knew it!" I burst out.

"What?"

"Paul wrote about this in his diary. You told Paul about it the first time he slept at your place. But Paul wasn't sure you were serious. Do you remember, Petr?"

He nodded.

"So Paul said he'd look in his third diary. To see what he was doing that day."

"Yes, exactly."

"But since I've only found Paul's fourth diary, I haven't been able to check what it was he was looking at. Do you know what it was?"

Petr took a deep breath.

"Yes, Jonas, I know what it was. I remember it very well, though I haven't thought about it for a long time. Paul had noticed a stag beetle on the asphalt outside the refectory. A big stag beetle. But there was something funny about it, something wrong. I believe it was one of the wings. That's it. One wing was sticking out in some strange way. So Paul bent down to get a closer look. He let it crawl into his hand so he could look even closer at the wounded wing. And as he was standing there with his outstretched hand, looking at this stag beetle, it suddenly took off and flew away toward the large trees beside the parking lot." Petr paused. "He was so nice, Paul. I was standing on the gravel path, halfway to the parking lot, looking at him. I couldn't see the stag beetle. I was too far away. All I could see was Paul.

And his movements. How he stood there looking down at the ground, how he squatted without touching the ground with his hands. And then, how he stood up. He was holding the palm of his hand in front of his face. Like he was watching his own hand. And then suddenly he looked up at the sky, as if he were searching for something I couldn't see. And all the time, while he was following the flight of the stag beetle, he kept his outstretched hand close to his face."

Petr was looking at me. "You see, it was a spiritual experience. It was like watching a magic dance, a ritual ceremony. He was so beautiful."

And tears started to roll down his cheeks.

It was late at night, and raining when Petr drove me home.

"You're welcome to visit me anytime," he said as he turned out from the street where he lived. "If you feel like it. It wasn't as hard as I had expected. It was, in fact, rather nice to talk about Paul."

"I would like to come back."

He put on the car stereo and the sound from a lonely trumpet was mixed with the rain lashing at the windshield.

"Do you like jazz?"

I shrugged. "A bit. Daniel hasn't really got anything but jazz records, so I've heard quite a lot. Some of it I like."

"Daniel ..." said Petr. "Paul often talked about him. He was a childhood friend of your mother's, wasn't he?"

"Yes. Did Paul say much about him?"

"Well, maybe not that much. But he liked him."

"Yes, I know he did."

Petr laughed and turned toward me. "Is there anything you do *not* know?"

I thought for a moment. "Yes, rather much, actually. For instance, I do not know what Paul was thinking of while he was standing on that railroad track."

"Nobody knows what he was thinking of," Petr said. "Do you really want to know, Jonas?"

I shook my head. "No, I don't think I do. I like this image I've got now. Of Paul, I mean. I think I would like to keep it."

24

Petr stopped at the parking lot outside our house. Through the rain I could see the light from our kitchen window.

For a while Petr let the engine go. Then he shut it off.

I was sitting silently by his side. I hadn't even noticed his gazing at me.

"What are you thinking of, *klučina*?"

I started. "What did you say?"

Petr smiled. "What are you thinking of, Jonas?"

I shrugged. "I don't know. This and that. Nothing special."

The rain was still pouring. I could see someone sitting at our kitchen table, but I couldn't make out whether it was Father or Mother.

"You're not sad, are you?" he asked and touched my arm.

"Sad? No, not at all. Why should I be? I'm not sad. I just think it's all so very strange. Like a dream."

"How do you mean?"

I looked into his dark eyes. "I'm not sure. It's like … it's like everything's blurred, and I'm not really sure what actually happened, what's imagination and what's reality."

"You mean the things that happened to Paul, and the things happening now."

I nodded. "Sometimes it's like we're one and the same, Paul

and I. As if there's only one. And the things that happened to him are also happening to me. Only now, instead. Do you understand?"

"Not really," Petr replied. "Do you mean that the things happening to you now are repeats of what happened to Paul?"

I thought for a moment. "It's hard to explain. It's more of a feeling, a sad feeling. It's like I know more about Paul than I ought to. I know more than what I have been told. It's as if my picture of Paul is based not only on what others have told me and what I've read in his diary, but also on something else. As if there is another way. From Paul to me, I mean. A shortcut, in a way."

Petr nodded. "Yes. Perhaps there is a shortcut. Who knows?"

And he went silent. The rain slackened and soon stopped.

I took my bag and opened the car door.

Petr stretched out his hand and touched my cheek. "See you!"

I stood in the parking lot, watching Petr drive down the street toward the exit road.

I felt fragile. I was both happy and sad. Happy, because I had met Petr, sad—or rather melancholy—because I had no more clues to follow in my search for Paul.

Petr had been the last clue. Now it was only me.

I opened the front door. The apartment was quiet. I took off my jacket and my shoes and put the bag in my room. I could hear a soft rustling sound from the kitchen.

It was my father. He was reading a tabloid.

"Hello!" he burst out, surprised, when he saw me. "I thought it was Sara. She went over to Else's a couple of hours ago."

I sat down opposite him.

"Did you have fun?" he asked.

"Yes."

He put down his paper. "I didn't expect you home until tomorrow."

"Really? Well, we ... I hadn't really decided how long I was going to stay. Anyway, I'm back."

And so that strange feeling of emptiness which often appeared when Father and I were alone together returned. It was as if we didn't have anything in common. And I felt guilty in a way, as if it were my fault we didn't have anything to talk about, anything to say to each other.

We sat quiet for a while, waiting for something to happen. Then I stood up and went into the living room to call Daniel, and Father returned to his tabloid.

I was standing with the receiver in my hand, waiting for Daniel to answer. But he wasn't there.

I hung up and returned to the kitchen.

"No one home?"

I shook my head. "Would you like some coffee?" I asked, as I poured myself a cup.

"No, thanks. I'm fine. I just had some."

I could feel him looking at me as I took the hot cup into the living room.

A short while later he joined me and sat down in the chair.

"Perhaps we could go for a walk tomorrow morning," he said, "since you're home. The two of us. If you've got nothing else to do, I mean."

I looked at him. "Where would we go?" I asked, as if it mattered.

He thought for a while. "Well, I could show you that fox burrow where Paul saw the three cubs."

I almost spilled my coffee. "Do you know where it is?"

He nodded. "Of course. We were there together, Paul and I. He showed it to me some weeks after he found it. And we went there a couple of times more before …"

"Oh, I didn't know," I said and turned toward the TV and the photograph of Paul.

"I don't know if they're still using it," Father continued. "I never went there this spring. But it would be nice for you to see the burrow, wouldn't it? And that rock he climbed before he saw the cubs."

A soft breeze was stirring the white curtain in front of the open balcony-door. The light and shadow were reflected in the glass on my brother's picture, bringing him to life. He was looking at me, and he was smiling.

"Yes, that would be nice. That would really be nice," I said.

And my father smiled too.

THE CZECH WORDS AND PHRASES:

Petr je tady	Petr is here/Here's Petr
Mému malému Princi	To my little Prince
Tvůj milenec	Your lover
Ahoj můj bratře	Hi, my brother
Stává se smrtelně důležitym	He has become deadly important
O malém princi	About a little prince
Jdeš mi na nervy	You get on my nerves
Václavské náměsti	The Vaclav Place
Můj malý princi	My little prince
Hajej můj princi a spi	Hush, my prince, go to sleep
Jsou s tebou anděle tví	Your angels will be with you
	(The first lines of the Czech lyrics to Mozart's "Lullaby")
Tvůj anděl je s tebou	Your angel is with you
Krucifix	Crucifix (used as a mild curse)
Klučina	Boy

Thanks to Klára & Václav for checking my Czech. Tisíceré díky.

Thanks to my friends Tom Stuart & Glenn Rounds
for your comments and support,
and for all your help in correcting my English translation.

The phrase *"It's the time of the season, when your love runs high"* is the first line of Rod Argent's song "Time of the Season". The song was released by his group, The Zombies, in 1968 and became a hit the following year.